About the Authors

Frank Dirscherl is the author of many novels, including the Amazon bestselling *The Wraith* and *Sanderson of Metro,* as well as several short stories. His *The Wraith Dread Avenger of the Underworld* books have been enjoyed by readers all over the world.

A librarian with over thirty years experience, Frank has also worked at a book wholesaler, a specialist medical practice and as a tutor in the writing and producing of comic books. His interests include reading, traveling, politics, architecture and the environment.

Frank lives in the Illawarra on the south coast of New South Wales, Australia, with his wife and daughter, and is always working on his latest literary endeavors.

Ray MacKay is a freelance writer of prose and comics, as well as a huge fan of both. Ray is relatively new to the writing world, but is thrilled to have already had the opportunity to write for esteemed publishers such as Big Bang Comics, Eyrie magazine and Oniric Comics, among others.

Ray has been a fan of superheroes, horror and pulp fiction for as long as he can remember and is overjoyed that he now gets to write stories like those he grew up reading and loving.

Ray is currently studying for a writing degree at university, while simultaneously seeking out work prose and comics mediums. He hopes to at least pay some of his bills this way. He lives in British Columbia, Canada with a roommate who he can't believe still tolerates him.

GLOWING*EYES*MEDIA

Praise for *Sanderson of Metro*
Amazon bestseller

"Once shrouded in mystery, The Wraith's stunning origin is finally revealed. Dirscherl and Nash have written one hell of an adventure novel filled with myth, intrigue, and excitement. Highly recommended reading."
- A.P. Fuchs, writer, *The Axiom-man Saga*, *The Way of the Fog*, *Undead World trilogy*

"Recommended for Wraith and pulp hero fans."
- Leon Mallett, *Amazon*

"At the end of the day, this novel is a worthy addition to The Wraith's continuing story and a necessary purchase if you're a fan of the character. It's also just a flat out enjoyable reading experience."
- Marcus Bucklin, *Amazon*

"The story is well written, and the Paul Sanderson character fleshed out fairly well...I highly recommend this well written entry for all comic book fans."
- Virginia E. Johnson, *Amazon*

Praise for *The Wraith*
Amazon bestseller

"I love the coloring job and specially the 'glowing' eyes on the chest of the character."
- Guillermo del Toro, director, *Blade II, Hellboy I & II*

"I liked the story a lot... It's a very strong debut."
Steve Englehart, writer, *Detective Comics, The Avengers, Green Lantern*

"I have read the novel (I couldn't put it down)... It is amazing to see how her (Leena) character evolves from Part I to Part II. At first she appears as every other 'girlfriend' in an action film, but those twelve months that pass obviously change her as a person and I love the person she becomes: tougher, but still human."
- Amber Moelter, actress, *Catwoman: Copycat*

"I finished *The Wraith* book last night. I must say I enjoyed it quite a bit. The scenes kept playing in my head like a big budget Hollywood film. I mentioned earlier that I enjoy when the hero is put to the test physically and doesn't win the battle unscathed. Boy, (Frank) delivered that in spades!"
- Jeff Welborn, artist, *Nightmare World, The Wraith*

"Genius + sweat + dedication = hard hittin' hero action! Go Aussie!"
- Dan Lennard, writer, *People* magazine

"*The Wraith* is a wonderful throwback to the purple prose of the bloody pulps with a hero clearly descendant from the likes of the Shadow and the Spider. A fast, action-packed thrill-ride with great characters, both noble and villainous. Slam-bang kick off to a super new series. One I'm anxious to follow."

— Ron Fortier, writer, *The Spider, Brother Bones, Domino Lady*

"I became familiar with Frank Dirscherl's The Wraith from the comic book of the same name. When the first Wraith novel came out I just had to read it. I was not disappointed. The Wraith is a fast-paced thrill-ride. I'm looking forward to the upcoming sequel."

— Bobby Nash, writer, *Evil Ways, Fantastix, Lance Star*

"*The Wraith* (is) a really fun read. Have been a fan of Kenneth Robeson's Doc Savage and The Avenger books for years... *The Wraith* reminds me of Robeson at his best."

— G.R. Lawson, Publisher, General Jinjur Comics

"A short, pulp, superhero novel... Clearly more adventures to come with how this is set up."

— Richard Scott, *Super Reader* website

"*The Wraith* is an enlightening journey into the darkness of superhero fiction, and a worthy entry into both pulpdom and comicdom."

— Kevin Noel Olson, *Silver Bullet Comics* website

"*The Wraith* is a testament to Frank's dedication and talent. Other small press characters have come and gone, but The Wraith endures, because Frank understands what makes a classic character."

– Richard Evans, writer, *The Canadian Legion*

"When it comes to superhero fiction and classic pulp stories, Frank Dirscherl channels those classic adventures of the past into *The Wraith* with ease and gives you a hero to believe in."

– Stephen J. Semones, writer/director, *Beyond the Lens, Crossfire, The Wraith: Eyes of Judgment*

"Frank Dirscherl's writing is action-packed and reminds me why superhero fiction is so much fun in the first place!"

– A.P. Fuchs, writer, *The Axiom-man Saga, The Way of the Fog, Undead World trilogy*

"Totally enjoyed this book. Good story, a real hero vs villain yarn. Can't wait to read the other adventures of The Wraith."

– J. Newey, *Amazon*

Praise for *Valley of Evil*

"The second Wraith novel is an improvement, I think. Right from the start Dirscherl throws you into the middle of crazy action.... This book is a whole lot of superheroic pulp fun, and the good news is there seems to be more to come...I look forward to some more of the same."
        – Richard Scott, *Super Reader* website

"I think (Dirscherl) really captured a noir element with (his) voice."
    – Joshua Gamon, writer, *Abigail & Rox, Digital Webbing Presents*

"I did quite enjoy the books. Best of all, it wasn't overly sex-filled or gory—I can't stand most modern superhero comics that show such things or have the heroes just swear and swear. So *The Wraith* (and *Valley of Evil*) was just up my alley."
    – Greg Gick, writer, *The Werewolf of Rutherford Grange, Tales of the Shadowmen, Secret Agent X Vol. 2*

"The Dread Avenger is back. After battling the Cobra in his first prose adventure, The Wraith returns to face all new challenges from Metro City's greatest villains, most notably Hong Kong drug kingpin Ma Tzi. As with his first Wraith novel, Frank Dirscherl treats us to a pulp-inspired adventure that keeps readers on the edge of their seat. You have to read this novel in one sitting."
    – Bobby Nash, writer, *Evil Ways, Fantastix, Lance Star*

"In the past five years there has been a tremendous resurgence in pulp fiction centering on the old heroic pulps. Young writers have started taking up the mantle of old masters like Walter Gibson and Lester Dent and begun creating their own avengers in tales of genuine purple prose. Among the best of this new generation of wordsmiths is Australian, Frank Dirscherl and the exploits of his modern pulp paladin, The Wraith. This is grand pulp!"
 – Ron Fortier, writer, *The Spider, Brother Bones, Domino Lady*

Praise for *Crossfire*

"Stephen did a fantastic job of bringing Frank Dirscherl's character to life!"
- Adam DiTroia, composer, *The Wraith: Eyes of Judgment*,
MTV, Fox Sports

"Loved the book!! Can't wait for the next installment..."
- Larry Mainland, actor, *The Walking Dead, Lawless,
The Three Stooges*

"The action comes swift, and doesn't stop until the final pages. *Crossfire* tells a great story of betrayal and revenge."
- C.R. Blevins, writer, *A Western Tale*

"This was my first introduction to The Wraith and I was not disappointed. The action comes swift, and doesn't stop until the final pages.... If you love a good action/hero story, you will certainly enjoy reading *Crossfire*."
- Ally, *Amazon*

"Makes me want more...should be the next series on Netflix..."
- Bill Lancaster, *Amazon*

"Another excellent entry in The Wraith Adventures series. Thoroughly recommended for Wraith fans and fans of pulp super-heroics."
- Leon Mallett, *Amazon*

Praise for *Cult of the Damned*

"Only by the first three pages, Frank Dirscherl wonderfully captures a dark and mysterious atmosphere, one that leaves the reader with a cryptic and eerie sensation; one that makes me cold just thinking about it."

> – Rennie Cowan, writer/director, *The Thriller Idol: A Tribute to the Legacy of Michael Jackson, Kade the Conqueror*

"Frank Dirscherl pulls you into the world of The Wraith from the first sentence and refuses to let you go until the last one."

> – Stephen J. Semones, writer/director, *Beyond the Lens, Crossfire, The Wraith: Eyes of Judgment*

"The Wraith is one of my favorite characters and every time Frank Dirscherl puts pen to paper I know I'm in for a real treat."

> – A.P. Fuchs, writer, *The Axiom-man Saga, The Way of the Fog, Undead World trilogy*

Praise for *Cry of the Werewolf*

"Frank Dirscherl delivers beyond measure.... The solid characters, settings and story really propel you page to page and leave you hanging on for more."

— Stephen J. Semones, writer/director, *Beyond the Lens, Crossfire, The Wraith: Eyes of Judgment*

"Each new installment in *The Wraith Adventures* series is a guaranteed good time filled with high adventure, romance and pulpy fun. Dirscherl is at the top of his form."

— A.P. Fuchs, writer, *The Axiom-man Saga, The Way of the Fog, Undead World trilogy*

"The writing is well done and well edited, and is filled with that distinct Dirscherl style of pulp that I enjoy so much. The book is a perfect example of what Neo Pulp/Superhero and Horror fiction can be and is a worthy addition to any fan's collection."

— Marcus Bucklin, *Amazon*

Praise for *Vendetta*

"...in all a great brew that had me hooked for the whole ride. Now bring on the next book, Frank..."

        – Leon Mallett, *Amazon*

"This book starts with a literal bang and doesn't let the foot off of the gas until the very last page. The book is well plotted and moves at a breakneck pace, making it an enjoyable, short read. I loved this book very much as a fan of The Wraith and I believe that anyone who is a fan of the series should consider this required reading."

        – Marcus Bucklin, *Amazon*

Praise for *Zombies Attack!* in *Metahumans vs the Undead*

"This compilation of superheroes vs evil offers top entertainment for superhero lovers! Frank Dirscherl and others are at their best with their contributed stories. I will now pursue other stories written by these authors, such as those involving Mr. Dirscherl's The Wraith. This type of reading enjoyment knows no end!"

—   Ramona Wingart, writer, *Where is Brother Beaver?*, *Emily Suzanne Smith!*

Praise for *Werewolves Attack!* in *Metahumans vs Werewolves*

"Always a great read. Can never put it down once you get started... "

– Geraldine L. Lewis, *Amazon*

BY FRANK DIRSCHERL

FICTION

The Wraith Dread Avenger of the Underworld series

Sanderson of Metro (with Bobby Nash)
Serpent Rising (with Greg Gick)
The Wraith
Valley of Evil
Crossfire (with Stephen J. Semones)
Cult of the Damned
Cry of the Werewolf
Swamp Witch of Satan's Forest (with Ray MacKay)
Vendetta
Lady Wraith (with Adam Oravec) - COMING SOON

SHORT STORY COLLECTIONS

Metahumans vs. the Undead
Metahumans vs. Werewolves
Metahumans vs. Robots
Metahumans vs. the Ultimate Evil
Lance Star – Sky Ranger Vol. 1

NON-FICTION

The Wraith: Eyes of Judgment – The Official Script Book & Movie Guide
(with Stephen J. Semones)
The Hitchers of Oz
Beyond the Lens (edited)

www.glowingeyesmedia.com

SWAMP WITCH OF SATAN'S FOREST

The Wraith Dread Avenger of the Underworld #6

by

Frank Dirscherl & Ray MacKay

GLOWING EYES MEDIA
WOLLONGONG

GLOWING EYES MEDIA
PO Box 31
Wollongong NSW 2520

ISBN 978-0-6457475-5-3

PUBLISHED BY GLOWING EYES MEDIA, January 2025
www.glowingeyesmedia.com
FRONT COVERT ART by Anon
COVER LAYOUT AND DESIGN AND INTERIOR DESIGN by Frank Dirscherl
EDITED by AP Fuchs
FIRST EDITION

For more on *Swamp Witch of Satan's Forest*
visit www.glowingeyesmedia.com

Text set in Garamond-Normal. Printed and bound in the USA

NATIONAL LIBRARY OF AUSTRALIA

A catalogue record for this book is available from the National Library of Australia

The Wraith Dread Avenger of the Underworld series in correct reading order (including short stories)

So far...but the story goes on...

For my wonderful family, as always - FD

To my Mom...the greatest inspiration, editor and mother I could ever ask for. Thank you for everything you did to help me get this done and everything you do for me every day.
Love - RM

SWAMP WITCH OF SATAN'S FOREST

~ Prologue ~

The darkness was overbearing. It was hot, hotter than anything he'd felt before.

No, wait, he thought. *I* have *felt heat like this before. I* have been *here before.* His thoughts were a jumble.

"Forgive me, Lord," he cried out. "I have failed. Failed utterly . . ."

His words faded away as a mighty shape rose before him, its massive bulk emitting a fervent crimson hue. Dr. Satanish hacked and heaved as the foul stench from the mighty creature wafted toward him. In quick time, the creature appeared through the billowing smoky haze. Crimson in shade, its skin was scaly and covered in a thick sort of slime. Its forehead was adorned with two enormous horns, curling three times before coming together at a point, and from its lower jaw protruded two tremendous, glistening fangs.

"You dare face me now?" the demon boomed. "After failing to free me from this dreaded prison, you dare face me?" It snorted a fetid, pale yellow mist from its nostrils, completely enveloping Satanish, who could not help but purge instantly. "Gnat! Why should I not incinerate you where you stand?"

Satanish stood upright, wiped his mouth and realized he was bleeding from a wound above his right eye. His memory of what had occurred, of his failure to release his demon lord Sizzelak from his confines, his failure to defeat The Wraith and unleash his werewolf hordes upon the masses, fully returned to him. He did not relish the memory.

"My Lord," Satanish sputtered. "Give me another chance. I can still conquer in your name, lay the foundations for your future ascension. I have other plans brewing—"

In a lightning-fast move, Sizzelak lunged for Satanish with a clawed hand and harshly yanked him up into the air. Satanish grunted and struggled, but there was no escape.

"I am confined here for another millennia. You can do nothing to free me until the next Zenith of Akhtar. You are a mere human gnat. Your bones will long be moldering in the dust by that time," Sizzelak boomed.

Satanish coughed and hacked at the foul stench of his master's breath. "I can lay the foundations, put into place a long-term succession plan. Your followers will be ready for your ascension long after I am gone."

Sizzelak threw Satanish to the graveled ground with a snort. "Do as you wish. I grow weary of you and your machinations. Go!"

Satanish wobbled to his feet. The icy-cold touch of Sizzelak had burned him to his core. He wondered there and then if he would ever be the same again.

He moved to speak—but nothing came. In that instant, he found himself back in the underground cavern from which he had originally woken.

And where his nightmare had commenced.

He was momentarily disoriented. It was dark, with only the merest flicker of light coming from a torch in the distance. His soul felt a torment he had never experienced before. It was not just his failure in his mission. It had been the touch of his demon master. He wondered if he had been the only one to experience such a thing and live.

He took a few moments to catch his breath. His mind went hazy. What had he just experienced? What was he to do next? Everything was a whirl. He clutched at his forehead, the blood still trickling from the wound. Every part of his body ached. He had somehow survived the bomb blast, had somehow made his way to the cavern entrance and crawled his way to safety. He had no memory of anything further than that. Or perhaps it was the—

Then he saw it...the wolf man who had attacked him on the school roof. It lay there a few feet from him in the low light. Was it unconscious? Dead? Had the creature, for some indiscernible reason, saved him and brought him to safety? He didn't know.

One thing he did know was he had to flee. Sooner or later, The Wraith or the authorities would come there in their search for a body or evidence of his escape. He had to move quickly. And formulate a new plan. Sizzelak would not regret sparing his life, Satanish vowed.

No, he would not regret it at all.

*   *   *   *   *   *

Paul Sanderson and his girlfriend Leena Patterson walked away from the still-smoking ruins of the Pondworthy School for the Mentally Disabled toward their badly beaten-up Bentley Continental GT car. His right arm was bandaged and held in a sling from the deadly war he and his team had just faced—a countryside of werewolf-like creatures, led and created by the nefarious Dr. Satanish, or "Dr. Roger Standish" as he had previously called himself.

Upon reaching the car, Paul turned and gazed back toward the destroyed school. Satanish had, apparently, perished at the hand of one of his own monsters, a wolf man who lunged at Satanish in vengeance at his plight. The mad doctor then detonated a series of explosives, leveling the entire complex, and themselves, with it. However, no bodies were found, no evidence existed they had indeed died as Paul and Leena had witnessed. It all felt too convenient. Someone like Satanish would have had some sort of escape prearranged, a Plan B as it were.

"I know what you're thinking," Leena said, no doubt noticing the look of consternation on his face. "We've just been over this. Satanish is dead."

"You really believe that?" Paul said, turning to face his beautiful girlfriend. "I don't. I want to, but I don't. I can't."

Leena sighed.

"I know, I know," he said. "I need to let go. Maybe I can, in time. Maybe I can."

They both entered the battered car. Paul sat there, stony-faced for a few moments.

"Where to now then?" Leena asked.

"John Ryan's house. I need some rest...and time to think."

* * * * * *

With all his strength, Satanish dragged the creature along the dimly-lit path. The wolf man was still alive, but just barely. It had a garish wound to its sternum, the blood still flowing freely. Satanish did not know how many of his creations were still alive, if any, so the importance of keeping this specimen viable was invaluable. True, the creature had turned on him, causing him to lose the final battle in his war on The Wraith, but it mattered little now. It was integral that he get the creature back to his underground safe house, a place no one knew about save himself. There he had a small, but handy, laboratory and could begin the rebuilding phase of his plans in secret, starting another army of human-wolf hybrids, perhaps even start experiments with other animals. He had always considered vultures a potential suitable sample.

At last, after much exertion, traversing the various darkened tunnels, Satanish reached his destination. Little more than a cul-de-sac, his safe house was not much wider than the tunnel he had used to reach this place, and was filled to the brim with scientific equipment of all shapes and sizes. Computers, scanners, beakers, vials, test tubes, and myriad shelves lined with books of every shape and size were crammed into this space.

Plopping down in a small chair, Satanish breathed heavily. He wasn't built for such intensive labor. He allowed himself a few moments of rest, but only a few. Soon, he was up, restrained the unconscious creature as best he could, and began collecting the equipment needed to begin his army of horrors anew.

* * * * * *

Paul and Leena made their way into the farmhouse that had once belonged to John Ryan and his family. Ryan had been, perhaps, the saddest victim of Satanish's plans for conquest. Paul could only wonder at the pain he must have experienced to have gone along with Satanish's ideas. Or he was tricked perhaps—at least partially—into the scheme. There was no way of knowing for sure. He only hoped that God would forgive the man his incredible sins.

"Ugh." Paul groaned, his wounded arm still causing him great pain.

"We never should have gone back to that school," Leena said. "There was nothing to be gained by going there."

"Enough," Paul said firmly. "I had to see the ruins for myself. I'm fine, really."

She looked at him with deep concern in her eyes, but said nothing more on the subject.

They made their way to the main bedroom of the house. The large queen-sized bed beckoned to him; he hadn't slept in more days than he could remember. Sitting down, he looked to Leena and realized that she, too, hadn't slept much in the past few days.

"Lie with me," he said.

She joined him on the bed and the two just lay there, finally allowing themselves some time to unwind.

And sleep.

* * * * * *

Satanish worked with fervor, extracting blood and skin samples from his creation, then analyzing and synthesizing those. He wanted to recreate the means to rebuild his lost army of animal hybrids, particularly the human-wolf specimen. But, in doing so, he would regain the building blocks to be able to extend those techniques toward other animals and thus increase the potential for his army. His records had been lost in the explosion so, while he retained much by way of memory, much was also written down on papers, computer files, and thus the hard work had only just begun to recover what had been lost. And at that moment, time was against him.

"Grrrrggh..."

A grumbling came from the creature, who appeared to be slowly regaining consciousness.

No, Satanish thought, *it's too soon.*

Before he could react, the wolf man was awake and struggling against his flimsy bonds. Satanish staggered backward as the creature broke free and stood, emitting an otherworldly howl, then remained still and defiant, staring him down.

"Stay back," Satanish said, brandishing a large syringe, the only thing akin to a nearby weapon. "Stay back, I say."

The wolf man snarled at him, but didn't move an inch closer. He wondered what the creature's next move would be?

With another snarl, the wolf man turned and loped into the receding darkness.

Satanish moved to intervene, to do something, but he knew it would be for naught. How could he stop the monster from doing as he pleased? In truth, the wolf man could tear him limb from limb. And, while he would have liked to have obtained more cell samples, Satanish believed he had enough to be able to continue with his work.

But, he needed to move quickly. He needed to obtain the results necessary and then make notes of the exact steps taken to achieve those results. And then he needed to remove himself from the area. With the wolf man again at large, he could no longer remain there. He would need to establish a new beachhead to begin the rebuilding phase and to launch future attacks.

The world would be his, he vowed. And Sizzelak would rise again. This was his solemn promise.

*   *   *   *   *   *

Paul awoke with a start. His brow was moist with sweat. He must have been dreaming, though he knew not what of. He checked his battered, but still functioning, watch. He'd been sleeping for hours. He looked to his beloved Leena by his side. She didn't stir. Feeling somewhat irritable and uncomfortable, he stood and left the bedroom. Standing in the home's small living room, he looked about him, noting the family photos and keepsakes of someone else's life.

Despite feeling better from the rest, he still didn't think the situation was over. Something gnawed at him, though he didn't know what, something….Deciding he needed some fresh air, he grabbed his coat and wrote Leena a short note of his intent.

Is Satanish truly dead? he thought as he wandered through the fields close to the farmhouse. He wanted to believe Leena, wanted it to be true, but what was this feeling hammering away in his skull? He couldn't discern the sensations. Call it intuition, call it instinct, but something was amiss.

He just didn't know what.

Before too long, he found himself in the charming little town of Bidbury. He'd wandered a little further than he'd wanted. The streets were deserted, the townsfolk mostly still evacuated due to the crisis. Without looking further at the town's beautiful buildings, he checked his watch and thought it best to get back to Leena lest she worry. As he turned to do so, an awful sound greeted him. He whirled to see a wolf man running up the main street, shrieking and grunting his presence.

"Oh no," Paul said.

He thought he had seen the last of these dreaded creatures. Could this mean more had survived, that more had not been cured? The thought brought shivers down his spine, but now was not the time for thinking. Action was needed.

Paul raced forward to meet the wolf man's onward march.

"Creature," he boomed in The Wraith's deep, ethereal tone, "halt there. You will go no further."

The wolf man lurched to a stop. It appeared enraged though somewhat confused.

"I can help you," Paul began. "My Judgment Stare can end your pain and bring you back to the path of good and right."

He moved forward slowly, trying to gain the creature's confidence. As he did, the wolf man lashed out, swinging its arm, seeming to intend a clawed hand to bury itself in his torso. Paul managed to dodge the blow. It was clear the wolf man had no intention of surrendering.

"I don't want to hurt you," Paul said. "Please, just let me help you."

The wolf man shrieked and renewed his attack. The creature, with claws at the ready, swung with one powerful arm and then the other. Paul managed to evade each attempted blow, but he was still injured and still tired. How long could he withstand such a ferocious attack?

He managed to connect with a strong left to the wolf man's jaw, but that only seemed to enrage the creature further. He connected again with another left, this time harder, and the creature flailed back. Paul noted the wound on the wolf man's back. This *was* the creature he had faced before, the monster that had assaulted Satanish on the school rooftop. He had to somehow communicate with him, ask him about Satanish. Using the Eyes of Judgment was no longer an option.

The wolf man lashed out once again, this time catching Paul squarely in the midriff. His thoughts of Satanish had distracted him, and he'd just paid the penalty with a gash to the midsection that now profusely oozed blood.

He managed to keep his distance from the wolf man's deadly claws, but as they circled each other, readying to continue their battle, he knew there was nothing else for it. He would have to go back to his original plan: Cure the creature with his Judgment Stare.

Without further thought, the Eyes of Judgment powered to life, crackling an eerie, fiery yellow energy.

"Pitiful creature," Paul boomed, "immerse yourself in the energies of the Eyes of Judgment...and be reborn!"

Paul rushed forward, catching the wolf man off guard, and enveloped the creature in the full power of the Judgment Stare. The creature moaned and writhed about, but was unable to break free from its thrall. The wolf man continued to struggle, to fight the power of the Judgment Stare, but it was of no use. Soon, his form began to change, the hair on its body began to recede and, a few moments longer, appeared human once more. What had once been the wolf man was now a young man with blond hair. He dropped to his knees and fell on his side.

"There, there," Paul said, crouching down and helping him sit up. "You'll be fine in a few moments."

Looking up, he saw some people slowly coming toward them in the distance and he thought retreat would be best. How could he explain what just happened?

He gently laid the boy down and jogged down the street in the opposite direction. Despite his exhaustion, he knew he'd be back at the farmhouse soon. It couldn't come quickly enough, for he had something to talk to Leena about, something he'd wanted to ask her for a very long time–since before he had become The Wraith–but the events of the past few days had coalesced those thoughts more vividly and now he was ready to put them into action.

He would ask Leena to marry him.

~ Chapter 1 ~

The air was crisp and clean. The sun glowed like molten gold on the surrounding countryside. A slight breeze curled its way through the branches of the nearby elms, birches and oaks. Some deer were spotted, feeding in an emerald-green field of tall grass. Fish darted here and there in the various streams, all of which ultimately snaked back through the countryside to the River Colin. As Paul Sanderson, his right arm in a sling, and Leena Patterson strolled through this marvel of nature, Paul could only shake his head at the horrors that took place in the surrounding area a mere few days earlier. And the instigator of it all, Dr. Satanish, had seemingly perished by his own hand. However, no body was found, so the question of his survival kept gnawing at his insides.

"What are you thinking, darling?" Leena asked, her beautiful face contorted in concern for the love of her life.

"All this incredible beauty," he started, "and yet Dr. Satanish eluded justice."

Leena brought him up short, stood in front of him, looked first at his wounded arm, then up into his eyes. "We've gone through this for days now. He died in that inferno. You saw it for yourself," she said softly. "He's gone. It's time for you to let go."

Paul gazed into her luminous blue eyes. They fairly sparkled in the radiant sunshine of the warm, spring day. "He appeared to perish, that's true, but there was no sign of his remains. He could still have arranged the whole thing. Faked his death somehow. The wolf man survived, after all."

"That's true," Leena said, "and you then dealt with the creature, but...even if you're right, say Satanish did survive, and got away—what can we do about it now, this very second? He's covered his tracks and is long gone by now."

He averted his eyes from her. The pain of the horror they had recently experienced weighed heavily on his shoulders. On his soul. So many lives lost, so much misery. Yes, Satanish's plot to raise his demon lord had failed. Yes, Paul had stopped the army of werewolves that had rampaged throughout the countryside, murdering at will. In all truth, they had won. So why did it feel to him like anything but that?

"We defeated Satanish, we destroyed his horrific experiments," Leena said. "And those that survived and were cured have no memory of what occurred. Our secret is safe." She smiled. "And we have each other, as always. You must find solace in that."

She embraced him carefully and, as she did so, he caught sight of the impressive diamond engagement ring on her left hand, dazzling in the sunlight. He had proposed to her the night before and she had eagerly accepted. Despite the incredible losses the area had experienced, so many lives *were* saved. Goodness knows the further terror Satanish would have inflicted upon the world had his obscene plot succeeded. And now they had further dedicated their lives to each other. In that regard, all was well.

"I love you, Leena," he said as his lips touched hers. Time stood still for the moment.

"I love you, too."

They started again, making their way back to the farmhouse of John Ryan, one of the conspirators in the heinous plot hatched by Satanish, and one whom did not survive the crisis. The home had been their refuge in the aftermath of their incredible battle to save mankind since their hotel had been decimated by the werewolves.

As they rejoined the path that connected the small town of Bidbury to their former hotel, crossing through Ryan's land in the process, Paul looked over his soulmate.

"You're right. I need to let go." He paused and looked at the beautiful countryside around him. "You still have several days leave from the library. Why don't we stay here, try and relax a little and maybe help start the rebuilding process with the locals?"

Leena smiled. "I was thinking along the same lines."

A few more minutes of walking and they reached Ryan's property. They clambered over the small ladder attached to the fence and plopped themselves down in the tall grass of the pasture on the other side. Butterflies and dragonflies swirled around them. Birds flew in the sky above and chirped from nearby trees. If not for the horrors of the last few days, Paul would have thought this was Heaven on Earth.

Perhaps it was, now that the evil of Dr. Satanish had been vanquished.

* * * * * *

Upon reaching the comely farmhouse, they entered it and sat themselves down on the small, fabric couch.

"Thirsty?" Leena asked.

"Mm...yes."

She stood and moved over to the compact kitchen, producing a jug of lemonade from the fridge. She had made the delicious, refreshing drink earlier that morning in the hopes she and Paul could now relax and enjoy their engagement. She hoped he would have asked her to marry him while they were there on vacation, and was relieved that, despite the events of the last few days, he still went through with it.

She gazed down at her ring, a three-stone diamond ring that was both subtle and extravagant at the same time. It was certainly the most elegant thing she had ever seen. But she was determined not to let the recent tragedies mar this special time in their lives. She mourned for the loss of life, of course, and felt terrible that more could not have been saved. She realized though, all too well, how many more lives would have been lost if not for their actions in stopping Satanish and his monsters. Paul's idea of staying on there, of assisting with the beginning of the reconstruction of the area, was just perfect.

"Thank you, darling," he said, receiving his glass and taking a long sip of the sweet drink. "Mm...perfect."

She sat next to him with a glass of her own, taking a nice, long sip herself. She took a deep breath. It *was* hard to relax, she realized. How did you wind down after what they've been through? What they've seen? She leaned against Paul, trying her best to put it all behind them. She looked down to her ring again. It really was the most perfect piece of jewelry she'd ever seen. She wondered, though, when they would ever find the time for the wedding?

"I'm a little tired, darling," Paul said. "The medication Dr. Trevalian gave me sure does knock me out. I think I'll take a nap."

"Of course," Leena said softly. "Rest, relax. Heal."

Paul smiled, gave a quick peck, and retreated into the bedroom.

Taking another swallow from her glass, Leena leaned back on the couch and momentarily closed her eyes. It was getting late in the afternoon and she thought perhaps a nap might not be a bad idea herself. Putting the glass down on the simple, pine timber coffee table, she put her feet up on the couch, stretching herself out nicely. If they were to start assisting with the rebuilding process the next day, perhaps it was only right they got some early rest.

She closed her eyes and soon dreamed of their impending nuptials.

*   *   *   *   *   *

The morning sun broke through the bedroom window, shining right on Paul's face. He stirred, rubbed his eyes, stretched out his good left arm.

That felt good, he thought.

He checked his Christopher Ward C60 Trident automatic watch. It had taken a beating through the recent crisis. The crystal was cracked, the steel bracelet was scratched and bent in places. But it still worked.

10 A.M. He'd slept for eighteen hours. He obviously needed the rest, for he felt completely refreshed and revitalized. Even his injured right shoulder felt all the better for it. He tried moving it. There was still some pain there, but there was also movement, much faster than the doctor had indicated there would be, but then the doctor had no idea his body healed faster than a normal man. Several times faster, in fact.

Leena was not in bed alongside him, and it was then he detected some wonderful aromas wafting in from elsewhere in the house. He sniffed eagerly.

Mm...bacon, sausage.

He strode from the bedroom into the living room and around the corner into the compact kitchen. Leena was there, sexy in her T-shirt nightie, cooking up a storm on the stove.

"That smells wonderful," he said, just then realizing how famished he was.

"I've got eggs, bacon, sausage. English style, of course. Tomato, mushrooms."

"It all looks and smells delicious."

He reached around with both arms and embraced her.

"Hey, be careful with that arm of yours," she said. Then she realized what he'd just done. "You...you have full movement already?" She spun on her heels.

"Not full movement, but it's already much better than even yesterday," he said, smiling. "You let me sleep an awfully long time."

"Looks like it did you the world of good. You looked so peaceful when I checked in on you. You obviously needed the rest."

"Obviously," he said, sitting himself down at the modest kitchen table. "How long have you been up?"

"A little while. I didn't need quite as much sleep as you," she said, winking at him.

She brought over two full plates of food and joined him at the table.

"Mm...it tastes as good as it smells," Paul said, eagerly cramming the food into his mouth.

"You're acting like you haven't eaten in a week."

"It feels like I haven't."

She smiled, and he could tell she knew just what he meant, that she no doubt got little sleep or nourishment either during the crisis.

"You ready to hit the town this morning, see what we can do to help?" Paul asked, wolfing down his food.

"There's plenty of time for that," Leena said. "Just don't rush so much with your food."

"Yes, ma'am," he said with a grin, and slowed down a little.

In time, both had finished their meals and sat on the nearby couch, relaxing and letting their food settle.

"And you said Max or Simpson had no knowledge of anything happening to them?" Paul asked.

"None whatsoever. Neither had any memory of us trying to contact them or that they were out of contact for any length of time."

"Strange," Paul said wistfully. "I wonder if that's anything we need to concern ourselves with when we get back."

"I don't know," Leena said, leaning on his good shoulder. "Everything seems fine. Perhaps it's nothing."

Paul looked at her closely. Perhaps she was right. He smiled.

"You're probably right."

He glanced at his watch.

"Let's head into town. I want to have a word with Sheriff Anderson."

Opting to drive rather than walk, Leena guided their damaged Bentley Continental GT slowly through the narrow country lanes. The car still drove perfectly well despite the pummeled-in doors and the missing windshield, damaged in the recent war with Dr. Satanish's horrific monstrosities.

"I just hope it doesn't rain before we can get this thing repaired," Paul said in jest.

Some minutes later, they were parking in the driveway of the Bidbury Police Station, where the sheriff and his daughter Julie also lived in an adjoining cottage.

"Hope he's home," Paul said.

This wasn't just a social call, however, nor was it only to do with Paul's idea to help the town. He and the sheriff had gone through a lot together over the last week. They had battled monsters and lost friends. Most importantly, Anderson knew his secret, and Paul had to find out just where he stood in the matter.

They proceeded to the front door and rang the doorbell.

~ Chapter 2 ~

"**G**ood of you to come see me, Sanderson."

Paul and Leena were seated on the couch of the sheriff's modest home. It was much tidier than the last time they had been there and the front door had since been replaced.

"Not at all. How have you been holding up?" Paul asked.

"Not too bad. Not too bad. Got the place cleaned up. Julie's off catching up with some friends. Those that made it through this."

Paul noted the strength of the man. The sheriff may well have been an experienced officer of the law, but he hadn't been trained or experienced in dealing with the kinds of evil Paul and Leena faced on an almost daily basis.

"So, what are your plans?" Paul asked.

Sheriff Anderson leaned back in his chair. "I wondered when you'd get to that."

Paul looked a little sheepish. "Forgive me, Sheriff, but I..."

"You needn't worry. Your secret is safe with me. "We've been through a lot together. You're a good man, doing a good, tough job. I won't do anything to hinder or prevent that."

Paul and Leena both smiled.

"Thank you, Sheriff," she said softly.

Anderson returned their smile and much good feeling passed between them, all unspoken.

"As to my plans," Anderson said after a brief pause, "I still intend leaving this area. Julie feels even stronger about it than I do."

"We understand," Leena said. "There is such pain in this place now, though most of the town doesn't know it or remember much of it."

"I know. That's the strange thing about it. Even those knee-deep in the plot are completely in the dark about everything that happened these past few days. I bet they're wondering whatever happened to their leader."

"Know when you're leaving? Where you're headed?" Paul asked, changing the subject.

"I'll stay and help the town a little. Wait for my replacement to arrive. Other than that, I have no idea."

"Well, if you're ever looking for a helping hand, you know where to find me," Paul said, leaning forward on the couch. He handed the sheriff a card. "Contact me any time."

"Good of you. Mighty good of you," Anderson said, pocketing the card. "And what of you two? What are your plans? Back to Metro City, I suppose."

"Yes, but not quite yet. I thought we could try and help rebuild the town first. Do whatever we can at any rate," Paul said.

"Right," Anderson said. "We can use all the help we can get, I'm sure." Anderson's face lit up when he focused on Paul's wounded arm. "You weren't wrong when you said you'd heal quickly. That right arm of yours wasn't just dislocated. To be honest, I thought it was lost."

Paul moved his arm to show Anderson just how well he was healing. "All is well."

"Amazing," Anderson uttered, clearly impressed.

"Well, that's that then," Paul said, standing. "We'll see you around the town, shall we?"

"Definitely," Anderson replied, a big smile on his face.

He proffered his right hand. Paul took it in his and shook it.

Not too much discomfort there, he thought.

A bond had been established that Paul knew would never be broken.

Exiting the house, Paul and Leena walked to their car. She looked to him and beamed. "Where to now?"

"Let's take a walk through town. I want to get a proper view of what's needed here and how we can help."

Ambling down Bidbury's main thoroughfare, if one could call it that, the two made note of the selective damage done to the town. Every so often one could see evidence of the werewolves' rampage. Doors were missing, windows were shattered, timber walls were partially caved in. Interspersed with dwellings such as those were others that appeared completely undamaged. Those were the homes and businesses owned by those involved with Dr. Satanish and his nefarious plot. In amongst all that, the street was lined with stunning varieties of flowering cherry and magnolia, all fully ablaze in their colorful abundance.

"Looks like an earthquake hit this place," Paul said. "See how typical the damage is of such a natural disaster? Some houses feature very heavy damage, others nothing at all."

"If only we could convince the people here with no memory of what happened that it *was* only an earthquake," Leena said.

"Wishful thinking."

"Will they try and gather together again? Satanish's brethren? Try and reform their group without him?" Leena asked.

"No," Paul said firmly. "The cure Max concocted was akin to them being bathed in the cleansing energies of the Eyes of Judgment. Evil has been stricken from their hearts. Now only guilt, shame, and pain remains, though the exact cause of this will forever remain clouded to them. They will try and get on with their lives as best they can with that burden placed upon them."

"They got off lightly."

Paul raised an eyebrow at that, but ultimately agreed with her.

Reaching the furthest extent of the small town, they stopped and turned to face the direction they had come.

"Not much to this town, really," she said.

"It was a beautiful town," Paul said, "and it will be again."

Before Leena could say another word, he had pulled his cell phone from his pocket and dialed.

"Max. Paul. Make a sizable donation to the Little England Disaster Fund. Say...five million dollars. Good."

Leena whistled. "That's a lot of money."

"All worth it. I want this town back in the shape we found it in. Remember how we felt when we first arrived here? How lovely it all was? How lovely this town was? The Wraith isn't the only one that can do good for the community."

Leena hugged him. "You are truly something special."

"And John Ryan's house," he continued. "As far as I know, there are no other relatives, apart from Walter Ryan, who will be cared for elsewhere for the rest of his life. I want to buy it. Make it our home away from home. I want the holiday we started to have here to continue, on and off, for the rest of our lives. This is a special place. I don't want Satanish to ruin that. Otherwise, in one small way, he still would have won."

Leena appeared thrilled with that.

"Consider it a wedding present?" he finished.

She hugged him again; they kissed.

"Let's head back to the house," Leena said after a few more moments looking over the town.

"Not yet," he replied. "I want one last look at the Pondworthy ruins."

Leena rolled her eyes. "Oh no. Not again."

Paul looked her square in the eyes. "Humor me. I just want one last look. Then, never again."

"Fine. One last look."

*   *   *   *   *   *

Paul exited the car and strode toward the ruins of the Pondworthy School for the Mentally Disabled—the site of his final encounter with Satanish, who appeared to have perished at his own hands when he set off explosives throughout the building. Paul still had a nagging feeling there was more to it than that, that Satanish had somehow faked his own death.

The wolf man had, after all, survived, and would have continued to terrorize the countryside if Paul hadn't stopped and cured him some days back. If the creature had escaped the blast with his life, why not Satanish?

And yet, they had found no evidence of this. No evidence he had survived the explosion. Someone as clever as Satanish undoubtedly would have been able to destroy any such evidence, and that was something Paul needed to keep at the forefront of his thinking. He knew to be conscious of his gut feelings, and this was one he couldn't shrug off.

"What did you hope to find here that we didn't find before?" Leena asked, coming up beside him.

"I don't know," he said, shuffling in the dirt. "A feeling, maybe. Some sort of impression, perhaps. I honestly don't know."

Leena turned him round. "It's over. You have to let go."

"In a way, I have. Trust me, I have. You're right. It *is* over. But..." He paced in a small circle for a moment, gathering his thoughts. "Think about it, though. Satanish was too smart to have been caught napping like that. He wouldn't have allowed himself to be caught in such a position, and he certainly wouldn't have ended his life willingly. I just know it. The wolf man survived, so did Satanish. I'm sure of it."

"You may well be right," Leena admitted, sighing. "There could be some truth to what you say. But, as I said before, what can we do about it now? There's no sign of him. If he escaped, he's well away from here by now."

"I know it. And yet..." His voice trailed off.

What is that...sound?

He turned and walked away from the rubble and ashes of the destroyed school, out toward the estate's perimeter fencing.

"Darling?" Leena called.

He ignored her and kept walking away.

"Paul?"

He reached the tall, wire fence and peered through it. Beyond the estate lay thick woods, and beyond that the swamp surrounded by "Satan's Forest," as the locals dubbed it.

There it is again, he thought.

"Darling, what is it? You're worrying me," Leena said, standing alongside him and staring at him, though he barely noticed.

"Don't you hear that?"

"Hear what?"

He looked at her pointedly. "That...voice..."

Leena looked out into the woods, in the direction Paul was pointed.

"Paul...I don't know hear anything."

"It...*she's* calling me."

"She? What's going on here?" Leena asked sharply.

Paul continued staring out into the woods. He couldn't help himself. He felt sure he heard a sweet, lovely voice calling out to him. And he felt compelled to listen. As though he had to go there and be with...her.

"That's it, we're leaving," Leena said.

She grabbed Paul and dragged him from the fence. He thought to break free from her, to go out and answer the call, but as they walked further from the edge of the estate, the sound—*her* voice—seemed to lessen and he regained his composure. Soon, they had reached the parking lot and their car.

"What on earth happened back there?" Leena said, her face contorted with concern.

"I wish I knew," was all he could say.

He furrowed his brow, opened the car door slowly and slid inside. It was as though a voice had been talking to him. Calling him. A female voice, so beautiful, so melodic. He couldn't get it out of his head. Even now, he could still hear her words humming in his mind, though the spell—for what else could he call it—had since been broken.

Come to me, she had called. *Come to me.*

He tried to shake the voice from his head, then turned to face Leena. "But I'm going to find out."

~ Chapter 3 ~

"**I** need you here, Max."

They were back inside John Ryan's farmhouse. Paul sat at the humble dining room table, communicating with Max on his Dell laptop via a scrambled connection.

"Right away, Chief," came Max's typed reply. "Is there a new problem there?"

"Yes, I think so," Paul typed on the secure line. "I need your scientific expertise. Something...happened to me earlier today. Something I can't explain. Something even *you* may not be able to explain. But I want you here all the same."

"Understood. I'll take the jet and be there shortly. Out."

Paul logged off the laptop and closed it. Leena stood behind him. He turned to her; concern was still visible on her attractive features.

"Max is coming, I take it?"

"Yes. If we're ever going to find out what happened to me back at the school, we need him here."

She took a seat beside him. "You said you heard voices?"

"Just the one voice. A female. She was...captivating. Beckoning me to come to her. I had trouble resisting."

"I noticed," Leena said in a slight huff. "This reminds me of Natalya Blackova. She exuded some sort of pheromones, as I recall."

Paul looked into her blue eyes. "Yes. This does feel similar, I must admit. But nothing was heard when Blackova exhibited her powers. And this is so much more potent."

"But I heard nothing. Nothing at all."

"Strange. I've never experienced anything quite like it. It certainly bears investigation."

"Are you sure that's wise? And with your injuries, I..."

"First things first," he said. "I don't want to go barging into that awful area before speaking further with Max. It's treacherous there: swamp and quicksand. When I was there some days ago with Jim Stone, a peculiar feeling came over me. Maybe today's incident was related to that in some way. Or maybe it's somehow linked to Satanish. Perhaps Max has some ideas or can somehow prepare us. Either way, I want to be as well informed as I possibly can."

*　*　*　*　*　*

It was late in the day. A strong breeze began to pick up as Max exited the Falcon 500 jet at the Bidbury landing strip. Paul and Leena stood by the partially-destroyed aerodrome, watching as the Irishman came down the gangplank. While waiting, Paul saw the mound of dirt that signaled Stan the airfield caretaker's grave from the corner of his eye—another testimonial to the tragedy that had befallen the region. He waved as Max drew nearer.

"Chief. Leena," he said.

The burly Irishman, a shock of bushy red hair visible under his peaked cap as always, carried two hefty attaché cases.

"Good to see you, Max," Paul said, shaking his hand. "I see you brought your mobile lab. Good. The equipment in the trunk of the car was partially damaged with what we put her through."

Max craned his neck to get a better view of the car. "Nothing I can't fix." He smiled.

Paul slapped him on the shoulder, and the three of them made their way slowly over to the Bentley.

"She's mighty banged up," Max said, looking the car over. "Not to worry, I made provisions for your new ride."

"New ride...?"

A revving car engine diverted the trio's attention to the airfield driveway where a sleek, dark gray, almost black, sports car glided into what served as the airfield's parking lot.

"What is this?" Paul said, impressed, as the driver exited. It was Jim Stone, who smiled at the team from ear to ear.

"The Rolls Royce Wraith," Max began. Paul arched an eyebrow at the name. "The most powerful engine in the Royce fleet, 6.6 liter twin turbo V12. And with a few little gizmos of my own thrown in for good measure." Max beamed as he completed his salesman-like pitch.

Paul moved over to the new car, let an index finger slide along the curve of its body. "Magnificent. The best addition to the collection yet."

"Oh, I've got this for you, too," Max said as he produced from his pocket a new watch. "Your current watch has clearly seen better days."

Paul raised his arm and looked down at his battered C60.

"So I was right to bring this along: the Héron Marinor."

"You're psychic, Max," Paul said as he removed his damaged timepiece and handed it to him, who offered the new model in return. "This looks interesting."

"Robust, completely scratch-proof, highly water-resistant. Just what you need in your line of work."

"Feels good on the wrist, too," Paul said. "Fully kitted out?"

"With the usual refinements," Max replied with a twinkle in his eye. "I can go over them if you like?"

"Later," Paul said. "I need to debrief you as to why you're really here. Can we go somewhere else?"

Max nodded.

"Jim, could you take the Bentley away, and I'll be in contact shortly as to your next assignment," Max said.

"Pleasure to be of any help," the young man said.

With an exchange of keys, Jim was quickly gone, and the three were alone.

*   *   *   *   *   *

At the Ryan farmhouse, Paul, Leena, and Max sat in the home's compact living room.

"So, do you mind telling me what on Earth is going on here?" Max asked.

"I don't know. Earlier today, on the school grounds, I thought I heard a voice. Now I realize I wasn't actually hearing it, but nevertheless my head—my mind—was filled with her voice. Calling me, beckoning to me. I found it difficult not to answer the call."

Max raised an eyebrow at that but said nothing initially, clearly thinking. After a few moments, the Irishman opened his two cases and set to work. He conducted various tests on Paul in an attempt to ascertain if there was any physical evidence to account for Paul's recent experience. Was he drugged? Or were there any chemical agents involved? No matter what, Paul was determined to know the truth.

"I can't find anything untoward in your blood," Max said sometime later after all the myriad of tests had been completed. He remained glued to his microscope. "No toxins, no chemicals of any kind that I can detect."

"I didn't think so or Leena might have been affected also," Paul said.

"Not necessarily," Max said, turning in his chair to face them. "It could be something along the lines of how Natalya Blackova affected us."

"You mean pheromones. Leena raised that possibility, also."

"That wouldn't explain the voice you heard in your mind," Max explained. "I was using that as an example of something being sex selective. As this could well be."

Paul stood up from the couch and began to pace along the front of it, rubbing his chin. "Then what *are* we talking about here? Telepathy? Some form of mind control?"

Max contorted his face in thought. "Possibly." He paused momentarily. "Yes, highly likely."

Paul continued pacing.

"Darling, you're beginning to wear a hole in the rug," Leena said, only half-joking.

"Could this have anything to do with Satanish or his cult?" Paul asked rhetorically more than anything else. "Or is this something else, something...more?"

He looked to Leena, who just stared back at him. Max merely shrugged his shoulders.

"Well, there's nothing else for it. I intend investigating the area."

"But, darling," Leena said, standing, "you're still not well enough. Your arm still hasn't healed properly, and your chest..."

"Leena, if this *does* have something to do with Satanish then I can't just rest, relax, and allow him to get away. Allow him to regroup and launch another attack on this country. Satanish or not, something is going on out there in the woods, something...evil. We cannot ignore it."

Leena looked to the floor. Paul knew she was aware of the truth of his words.

"I understand, but....I understand."

She touched his cheek with her left hand, caressed it softly.

"That...that ring," Max spoke up excitedly. "Are you? I mean, you're finally?"

"Yes, Max," Paul said, turning to face the Irishman, "we are indeed engaged to be married."

Max jumped to his feet. "That's wonderful!" He grabbed the two of them in his arms, embraced them in one giant bear hug. "Congratulations." He let them go and looked at them both keenly. "And about bloody time, too, if I may say."

"You may, and you're right," Paul said. "It was just about finding the right time. I'm not sure if that even truly exists these days, but I felt it was finally time."

Max sat back down in his chair, his various scientific equipment littering the coffee table behind him. "That's wonderful. You kids deserve it, deserve every happiness."

"Thank you, Max," Leena said, a big smile on her face, which slowly vanished when she turned to face Paul.

"Tomorrow morning," he said, "we begin to find out what's going on here."

~ Chapter 4 ~

The Rolls Royce Wraith skidded to a halt in the parking lot of the still-smoldering ruins of the Pondworthy School for the Mentally Disabled. As the trio exited the super car via its *suicide doors*, Max looked up at the ruins, lifted his peaked cap slightly then whistled softly.

"Someone had a real go at that," Max said.

"It was over there," Paul said, ignoring Max and pointing to the edge of the lot, "where I was overwhelmed."

Max carried his attaché cases there and opened them, producing various intricate pieces of equipment. Paul and Leena watched as Max scanned and analyzed various air and soil samples in and around the area. Paul turned and gazed at the ruined school. A feeling of dread, of sheer apprehension, threatened to overwhelm him there and then, and it was then he knew his instincts were right. Satanish *had* somehow escaped. He didn't know how, he just *knew* Satanish was alive and at liberty. The thought brought shivers to his soul.

A stiff breeze had picked up, and it was overcast and cooler than in previous days. Leena moved to face him, her hair billowing in the wind. "What's on your mind?"

"You know what I'm thinking about," he said, smiling weakly. "Satanish is out there, somewhere. I let him escape."

Leena was about to fight that notion, when Max, now some distance away, turned to them. "I can't find anything unusual here," Max cried out. "Nothing at all."

Paul's eyes tightened. What was the next step?

* * * * * *

Before another word could be uttered, Paul's body went limp and his expression turned blank. As Leena watched on in horror, he started toward the thick woods that surrounded the school.

"That voice...so beautiful..." Paul said in a whisper. "I must go to her."

"Max," Leena shouted. "Help me drag him to the car."

The Irishman hurried over and took strong hold of one of Paul's arms. "Chief, you don't want to go there."

With Leena holding his other arm, Paul struggled to break free. "But I must. I must. She's calling me. She *needs* me. I must go to her."

"Chief," Max blurted, struggling to keep hold of him as he fought for release, "snap out of this. Focus on my words, not hers, whoever she is. Look at me, look into my eyes. Focus on my voice."

Paul, his face sweating profusely, his body trembling, managed to turn his head and avert his gaze toward Max.

"Good, good," Max said as he and Leena were now able to drag Paul away from the edge of the forest and back toward the car. "Listen to my voice. You are in control. Nobody else. You!"

As they reached the car, Paul's muscles seemed to relax, his breathing normalized, and Max and Leena were able to loosen their grip.

"It's okay," Paul said, taking a deep breath. "I'm okay. Thank you, both of you."

"The voice again?" Leena asked, concern building within her.

After a few moments, Paul said, "Yes, but so much more potent this time. She wasn't just calling me. It was as though my will was gone. Nothing was more important than going to her."

Max wiped his brow. "I'll bet nothing will show up if I take bodily fluid samples."

"Then don't," Paul said, placing his hands on Max's shoulders. "We need to take another tack with this."

"What do you mean, love?" Leena said.

"We need to make our way to Satan's Forest."

⋆   ⋆   ⋆   ⋆   ⋆   ⋆

Later that day the three of them marched through the woods on the other side of the Bidbury Court boutique hotel. Both Leena and Max wore knapsacks, filled with provisions acquired earlier from the village stores that were still open. Paul opted not to wear his Wraith uniform at this stage, even though Max had brought a pristine specimen with him when he arrived in Bidbury.

It was still overcast, with inclement weather a distinct possibility, and a cool northerly wind had picked up substantially. The conditions lent their surrounds a gloomy eminence. This was no longer the wondrous natural playground of the previous days.

"How long do you think it'll take us to get there?" Leena piped up above the din.

"A few days, maybe. It's hard to say. Weather could play a part as well," Paul replied. "It would have been faster had we headed there from the Pondworthy side, but I thought approaching the site from this side, while a longer route, might hold off that...influence somehow."

He looked down at his Marinor watch. It was getting late in the afternoon. He wondered briefly if they should have delayed their journey until morning but, then again, there was no time like the present.

The group paused at the edge of the forest. The woodland area known colloquially as Satan's Forest seemed to beckon them forward. Paul felt an unnatural shudder run the course of his body. He knew there was something in those woods he would have to confront, though he wasn't sure he had the strength to do so. Yet, it wasn't like he had much of a choice.

Leena watched him take a deep breath, then take a strong stride towards the edge of the forest. She and Max followed him, sharing an apprehensive look as they did so, Paul noted.

The entrance to the forest, if you could call it an entrance, opened up like a massive jaw, its lips lined with trees and dense brush. The three disappeared into the forest's mouth, and the shade of the trees swallowed them whole.

*   *   *   *   *   *

Deep in the forest, far beyond where anything living dared tread, a haunting laugh emanated from an unknown, sinister place. It was almost as though something sensed The Wraith's entrance into the forest. Something old and evil and cunning. Something was pleased he had arrived. Something that had been calling to him. Something was waiting for him.

~ Chapter 5 ~

The tree cover in Satan's Forest was some of the darkest Paul, Leena or Max had ever experienced. Only the smallest and briefest glimpses of sunlight were visible through miniscule cracks in the foliage above. The trio had been traveling for about an hour and though it was still late afternoon, it appeared as if dusk had already settled into the woods.

The darkness of the forest wasn't the only contributing factor to the group's slow pace. Satan's Forest was virtually untouched since the Puritan times, and the trees and foliage grew in vast clumps that made any linear path difficult. There was a semblance of a trail here and there, possibly carved by some previous travelers, but it was always faint at best.

Paul still led the group, with a nervous Leena following and a concerned Max taking up at the rear.

Leena was uncomfortable with the group's plan. They knew very little about this forest, and even less about what was wrong with Paul. He repeatedly heard the voice of another woman calling to him and the voice's power troubled her deeply. It wasn't just the thought of her fiancé being obsessed with another woman: it was the idea that some sinister force might grab hold of him. The Dread Avenger was a powerful force, both physically and mentally, and if he was swayed to the side of darkness there was no telling what evil he could accomplish.

But there seemed no alternative except to seek out this strange voice calling to Paul and confront it—if that was even possible. They had to find out. So, she kept quiet about her apprehensions as she stepped over a massive fallen log.

The three continued on for another hour or so until night fell upon the forest like a blackout curtain. It became treacherous to follow the supposed path, even with powerful flashlights, so they decided to make camp for the night in a small clearing not much bigger than the floor space of an elevator.

Max started a small fire over which they cooked some vacuum-packed beef. The food was surprisingly good though not very filling. They ate with relish. The trip so far had been exhausting despite their extreme fitness, and all three of them were famished.

"How are you feeling, Chief?" Max asked after they had completed their meals. His question was obviously an attempt at subtlety and the concern in his tone was hard to miss.

"Fine, Max." Paul replied. "Really. Just a little tired, is all. In fact, I think I'll get some rest. We've got a big day ahead of us tomorrow."

Max nodded. "I'll take first watch."

Max looked at Leena as Paul slipped into a sleeping bag.

"You all get some rest now," Paul said.

Leena unfurled her sleeping bag and placed it next to him. She got in and after she zipped herself up, Paul put an arm around her shoulder.

"It's all right," he whispered. "I know you're worried, but I feel fine. We'll get to the bottom of all this."

"I'm sure we will," she whispered back, "but I'm just a little worried about what might be out there."

"I know how you feel," Paul said. "It's not like we haven't been through enough already."

"Do you think this has anything to do with Dr. Satanish? Or his werewolf creations?" Leena said.

"Anything is possible," Paul said. "After what we've just been through, common sense would dictate it likely. And yet..."

"And yet?" Leena said.

"I just don't think so. I don't know, call it a gut feeling."

She knew full well his gut feelings were usually spot-on. She smiled.

"Leena," he said as he turned her face with his hand. "Get some rest." He returned her smile.

She sighed, and turned over to try and let sleep take her in its grip.

* * * * * *

The Wraith found himself sprinting through the woods of Satan's Forest, chasing the dark figure ahead of him.

He had seen someone or something moving in the woods not far from their camp, but it had disappeared back into the dense brush before he could get a clear look at it. Now he found himself in fast pursuit of it, sprinting through the dark foliage.

The forest itself seemed to be trying to slow his hunt. Trees scratched at his face and hands, his feet stumbled over roots, and his cape snagged on thorns and branches. Satan's Forest was a much different battlefield than the streets of Metro City. But the Dread Avenger could—and would—adapt. He pressed on, his mighty legs pumping harder and harder until the distance between himself and the figure became smaller and smaller. He could almost make out the dark outline of a person, running through the forest ahead of him. Finally, he was upon the stranger, and reached out to grab at them. But his gloved hand snatched at empty air as the figure disappeared into the darkness. The Wraith tried to stop, to prevent himself from rushing blindly into the unknown ahead of him, but he seemed to have lost control of his own legs and continued his charge into the blackness.

Within moments, the forest floor seemingly disappeared out from under him and The Wraith found himself falling off the edge of a cliff. He let out a shout of panic and desperately twisted his body in mid-air, trying to grab at the edge of the cliff. His fingers found no purchase and he plummeted.

Down, down, The Wraith fell into the inky blackness. He fell end-over-end-over-end, completely disoriented until he splashed hard into a river below. His velocity plunged him deep into the icy water and he found himself deprived of all senses, running out of air in the dark, cold river depths. Desperately, he swam for the surface, but it never seemed to arrive. It was just endless water. He needed air. Suddenly, The Wraith burst upward, frantically gasping for sweet oxygen. He found himself engulfed in a raging torrent of whitewater.

The Wraith blinked hard, willing his eyes to adjust so he could take in his new predicament. The dark waters of the river pulled him steadily downstream to...what? He could see none of his surroundings; the only color that stood out among the blackness of the water was the white froth that churned around him.

A moment later, something stood out to him. Nothing more than an outline, but it appeared to be a branch of some kind. Summoning all of his strength, The Wraith lunged up, grabbed hold of the branch with one hand, stopping his downriver momentum. Sodden, he quickly looped another arm around the branch and pulled his upper body out of the river.

The branch shuddered and The Wraith thought it was about to snap and plunge him back into the raging water. But instead the branch moved unnaturally, retracting and pulling him up out of the water and onto the shore. And it didn't stop. The branch ripped itself out from under The Wraith's arms and coiled itself around his chest. It snaked its way down both his arms and yanked them up straight. The wood of the branch tore through his suit, cut into his skin like a rope made of sandpaper, as it bound him against the tree's trunk. More rope-like branches snapped tight and The Wraith closed his eyes and let out a groan of pain as his back dug into the rock-hard wood of the tree trunk.

A dazzling light burst through his closed eyelids. Wondering at their source, he cautiously opened his eyes. Slowly, letting just a thin sliver of light in–still blinding–and he needed a moment for his vision to adjust. He was no longer by the river's edge. The Wraith now found his arms bound by coarse ropes to a wooden pillar. His legs were also bound, and he was covered up to his knees in kindling and dry branches.

"Please don't," a voice cried out in horror. "I beg of you."

The Wraith turned to seek the source of the voice. There was a woman next to him, bound in a similar fashion. She had long, dirty blonde hair, and wore a tattered dress. Her face was stained with mud, blood, and tears. Next to her was another woman, also tied in the same way. And beyond there was yet another. And another. The line of imprisoned women seemed to go on far into the horizon.

"Shut your mouth, foul sorceress!"

The Wraith turned his attention away from the women to their captors. In front of them all stood half a dozen figures cloaked head to toe in black. Their gaunt faces were partially obscured by the shadow of the brims of their hats, but even the shadows could not hide the hatred in their eyes.

"We will not hear any more of your evil words," the apparent leader of the cloaked figures bellowed, stepping forward. "Prepare thyself for what is but a taste of the flames you shall writhe about in Hell!"

The Wraith's breath caught in his throat. He realized, much too late, that he and the other women were not bound to pillars. They were tied to stakes–and about to be burned at them.

A torch was thrown at The Wraith's feet and the kindling around him immediately burst into flames. He couldn't help but scream as the fire began to burn away at his legs and move upwards. The fire channeled up his body, burning away at his costume and then his flesh. The Wraith screamed, a primal, agonizing cry and it mingled and melded with the screams of the burning women around him. His mouth tasted blood while his nose filled with the horrid smell of boiling flesh. The chorus of screams was almost deafening, but one tone stood out among the others and was growing stronger. The woman to The Wraith's side wasn't screaming.

As the flames ate away at her flesh, she laughed, as if the entire ordeal was hilarious. The Wraith stared at her: she was horrified, confused and in unimaginable pain. Then she turned to look at him as her hair withered and turned to ash.

"You will be mine..." she screamed at him through melting lips. "You will be mine, Paul!"

"Paul!"

"Paul!"

"Paul!"

*   *   *   *   *   *

"Paul!"

"Paul!"

Paul woke with a start, sitting bolt upright. He looked around quickly, checking his surroundings. He was not bound to a burning stake. He was in the clearing where he and Leena and Max had made camp the night before. Both of them now stood over him, their faces portraits of concern and bewilderment.

"Paul..." Leena said.

"Chief?" Max said. "How did you..."

Paul tried to clear the cobwebs from his head. "I just had the most vivid nightmare. I've never experienced anything remotely like it. It was like...like I was reliving a memory or something. I can't really explain it otherwise."

Paul's explanation did nothing to ease Leena or Max's apparent concern. But it was Leena who finally asked Paul the blatantly obvious question: "Paul, when did you change into The Wraith?"

Paul finally noticed himself, put his hands to his head and felt the cowl in position there. And as he looked down, sure enough, he was now cloaked in the familiar black and blue suit of the Dread Avenger of the Underworld. He yanked the cowl off and looked at her. His feeling of bewilderment now mirrored hers.

"I don't know, Leena."

~ Chapter 6 ~

There was no rational explanation for Paul's change of wardrobe. As with many of the recent occurrences they had experienced, very little made sense, but they decided to press on. Potential answers lay forwards not backwards. He placed his cowl within his backpack while remaining suited up as The Wraith.

They had broken camp just after sunrise and pressed on into the depths of Satan's Forest, following the faded path as best they could. As they had discovered the previous day, the path through the forest was not a linear one. It wound and twisted, often wildly, and through foliage thick enough to almost require a machete to slip through it. As such, their progress was slow and arduous.

The storm that had threatened but not materialized the day before now seemed to come out of nowhere. The sky turned even darker in the blink of an eye and ominous clouds had gathered by the time Leena looked up at the angry-looking sky. Then the rain started. Light spattering of drops at first, but they soon increased, quickly turning to a mighty torrent.

Paul found himself grateful that his suit was, for the most part, waterproof. Leena and Max were left digging through their packs for camouflage rain ponchos.

As the three continued their trek, encumbered further by the downpour, the black clouds above let out a low rumble, like a tremendous waking dragon, which then began to spew forth lightning onto Satan's Forest.

Though it was clearly many miles away, the first lightning strike illuminated the forest before them, such was its intensity. It lasted only a precious few seconds then they were plunged back into the darkness of the raging storm.

Max shivered and pulled his poncho tighter around him. The rain seemed to pelt down with even greater intensity. Icy needles plunged down upon the trio in sheets. The water quickly began to soak through Leena and Max's ponchos and, though he would never admit it, even Paul felt the damp chill beginning to infiltrate his suit.

The storm filled the very air around them in an all-consuming chaotic inferno. "Paul?" Leena called out from the darkness behind him. "Where are you? I've lost sight of you."

"I'm right here, Leena." Even to his own ears, his voice almost sounded like it came from somewhere far away. Paul turned to where Leena had been walking just a moment ago, only to discover darkness. He reached out into the blackness, hoping to grasp the love of his life by her shoulder, her hand, anything.

But all he found was empty darkness.

"Leena? Max?" Paul shouted, reaching blindly around him, searching for his fiancée and his friend. Somehow they had disappeared into the pouring cold dark that surrounded him as though the storm had swallowed them whole like a gigantic creature. He thrust himself forward to where he thought they had last been standing, but again found nothing.

In his haste and worry, Paul snagged a foot on a stray root. He let out a yelp as he pitched forward and fell head over heels downward, careening down an embankment. Rolling over and over, his fall was brought to a sudden and painful halt as he slammed hard into something solid.

Paul felt several ribs crack against the side of what he now saw as a massive oak tree. He gingerly moved to one side, spat out a combination of mud, foliage and grit, and groaned. Then he slowly rose to his feet. With the raging storm and the thickness of the forest all around him, it was impossible to see anything. Then he remembered the night-vision lenses in his cowl. Thankfully, his backpack was still strapped to his back. He removed the cowl from it and placed it over his head.

The Wraith tapped at a spot on his temple and his night-vision lenses slid down into place within his cowl. The dark of Satan's Forest became almost as clear as day. The Wraith saw now the tree he had rolled into stood at the bottom of a rather steep hill. Below the tree there was a clearing and from there perhaps a way back to the path, back to Leena and Max.

The Wraith set out cautiously, making his way through the clearing. The path out of the clearing soon narrowed as he went along, The Wraith again having to contend with branches slapping and scraping at his broad shoulders.

His ribs ached, but he pressed on, ignoring the pain as best he could. Then, without warning, the path dropped off.

The Wraith barely had time to catch his breath as he plunged head first into a morass of murky mud and water. He made an undignified splash as he landed then quickly jumped to his feet, coughing up. Again, he found himself checking his surroundings after an unplanned spill.

The swamp itself was expansive, at least from what he could see of it through the rain and fog. Right now, his night vision lenses proved of little use. He turned around to check the direction he had come. It was a slippery, steep climb, and that continued to the left and right of his point of entry as far as he could see. So, forward, through the muck, appeared to be his only option.

He began to make his way as best he could through the swamp. It was slow-going; every step was like trudging through mounds of wet concrete that was on the cusp of hardening. To compound The Wraith's difficulties, tightly-packed mangroves sprouted up here and there, blocking his path, forcing him to sidestep them, entering deeper water, just to circumvent them.

Now I know why they call it Satan's Forest, The Wraith thought. *Walking through here is absolute hell.*

His thoughts turned back to Leena and Max; his mood soured further. Where were they? It was possible he was now moving in the complete opposite direction to wherever they were located, but he currently had no alternative to press on. He could only hope firmer footing would soon be at hand.

The Wraith suddenly thought he heard a faint...something, but it was difficult to ascertain through the din of the storm and the sound of his muddy plodding. As he continued his treacherous march, the sound–whatever it was–became more audible. A gurgling at first, then bubbles broke through the surface of the muck before him. The bubbles quickly increased in number and intensity, ultimately resembling the boiling of a pot on the stove. Ripples, resembling small waves, emanated out from the center of this foul cauldron.

The bubbling and boiling intensified and the muddy water began to churn and shudder as something began to rise from the watery depths. The Wraith could do nothing but stare in horror and confusion as an ominous shape pulled itself from the murky underbelly of the roiling swamp. The thing that rose up was caked in a thick layer of mud and plant-like debris. But as it slowly gained purchase–on what The Wraith could not even guess–and turned to face him, the torrential rain began to wash away the dirt and mud and The Wraith got his first good look at the thing before him.

The creature was a towering repulsive heap of muddy hair, with sticks and brush riddled within its coarse hide. It was at least seven feet tall, humanoid in shape, with arms and legs of tremendous size. Beneath a bushy brow of grass, The Wraith was shocked to see two gleaming red eyes staring back at him.

The heap seemed to have found some sort of footing in the swamp and now it stood knee-deep in the murky water, staring at him. A long, vine-like nose extended from between the creature's bulbous eyes, the nose pulsing intermittently, as though the heap was breathing through mossy lungs. Where a mouth would usually be found, there was a large gaping black hole.

The Wraith was speechless. He'd faced madmen, criminals–including the crime lord Robert Latham–cults, assassins, and now even werewolves, but yet he couldn't believe what he saw in front of his own eyes. As fantastic as the creature appeared, it was real, and had the foulest stench he had ever encountered. He couldn't help but wretch with every second breath.

The Wraith stared at the heap in front of him, taking in every grotesque detail of the swamp monster's murky and mucky frame. It stared back at him, as if equally transfixed by The Wraith's presence, surely an unwanted stranger in its eerie domain.

Then, the heap jerked its head and stared at The Wraith's chest. The Wraith realized it must have been the Eyes of Judgment on his chest that so captivated the creature.

The Wraith wondered at that, and decided to try something. The Eyes flared to life in electrical fury, bathing the area in a sickly, sinister yellowish hue. The swamp creature recoiled at the sight of the Eyes come to life, almost as though hurt by the purifying brightness. It let out a guttural howl and put its paws over its face in some form of defense. The Wraith deactivated his Judgment Stare.

The heap lowered its paws, and as it did so, the creature's dull red eyes were narrowed in what appeared a primitive rage. The creature let out an angry cry from somewhere within its body and then charged at The Wraith with a sudden speed, impossible within the swamp yet here it was. Its mossy legs caused massive splashes in the slop as it bounded towards him.

The heap charged at The Wraith and leapt at him, somehow able to catapult itself through the air. The Wraith was stuck fast in the mud, unable to move quickly. The creature slammed into the Dread Avenger, grabbing him in a bear hug, lifting him aloft and tossing him up and out of the swamp.

Firm ground at last.

Before The Wraith could gather his thoughts, the creature had joined him on land, reached out with a filthy paw, clenched its fist and launched its weapon at The Wraith's head. He ducked the blow, the fist continuing its deadly trajectory and smashing into the tree behind The Wraith, reducing it to splinters.

The Wraith somersaulted backwards in an attempt to put some distance between him and his enemy, perhaps to also catch it off guard. And it worked. The Wraith wrapped his cape around him.

"I mean you no harm," The Wraith said.

The heap's response was another inhuman roar as it rushed at The Wraith. This time, The Wraith stood his ground as the heap approached him, arms up, ready to attack.

Just as the heap got within striking distance, The Wraith threw open his cape and lashed out with a brutal uppercut. While the creature had strength and size to its advantage, The Wraith had guile and training. The creature let out another primal scream and reeled backwards, clutching at its face, likely more in shock than in pain. Then it turned back to The Wraith, pure hatred lighting up its hideous face.

The Wraith assumed a fighting stance and raised his hands, preparing for the next attack. The Wraith didn't have to wait long. The creature let out another roar and rushed at the Dread Avenger. The Wraith leapt to one side and quickly positioned himself behind the creature. He karate chopped with both hands into the sides of the heap's neck. It was a soft spot. The creature howled in pain.

With surprising speed, the heap whirled and caught The Wraith in his midsection with a clothesline attack. The air was knocked from his lungs as the blow sent him rolling through back into the swamp. His cracked ribs throbbed even more now.

Gritting his teeth in pain, The Wraith jumped to his feet just in time to sidestep another attack from the heap that now brought its paws down in a deadly swipe. But its aim was off, and ultimately the swipe did nothing but tear the bottom of The Wraith's cape.

The Wraith jumped out of the marshy ground, back up on to solid ground, and threw all his force behind a powerful right cross to the creature's face. The hit hurt the creature, but it hurt The Wraith more. It was like slamming a fist into a concrete wall. Pain or no pain, The Wraith immediately jumped back at the heap, delivering an equally powerful left hook to the creature's head. It hurt, but this time it hurt the creature more. It howled in agony and staggered back.

It was about time.

The Wraith watched on in horror as the creature stumbled back a bit. Its face was damaged, almost as though its skin was...loose? Another howl of pain, then the creature reached up and tore at the hair, moss and flesh on its face, stripping it to the bone. The Wraith couldn't help but gasp at the sickening sight before him. Its face–its skull–was clearly human in appearance. Its red eyes glowed with a malevolent energy, and it readied itself for another strike.

Again, the creature was upon The Wraith with uncanny speed. Without time to dodge or parry, the creature grabbed The Wraith in its powerful paws and lifted the Dread Avenger above its bony head. It let out a menacing growl. The Wraith flailed out with a boot, catching the creature with a mighty blow to its skull. The heap screeched and dropped The Wraith to the ground at the swamp's watery edge.

In an instant, the creature fell onto The Wraith. It grabbed hold of him with its mossy paws and began to push the Dread Avenger's head and torso into the murky depths. The Wraith barely managed to grab a breath before his head was pummeled into the mud and water. The Wraith thrashed about, trying to pry free of the heap's grasp. He grabbed hold of the mossy arms that held him underwater and tried desperately to move them, using what little strength he had left. But no matter how hard he flailed, the heap's hold on him remained strong. The Wraith started to lose strength. He was drowning.

No. It can't end like this.

He had one last chance. The Wraith scrambled to reach his belt. A flash pellet was his last chance at life. In desperation, he found it and managed to reach back and slam it into the creature's arm. The force of the pellet tore its right arm off. In truth, it disintegrated. The creature staggered back, in pain, in shock, and let out an unholy howl. The creature reached up with its left paw in search of the arm that was now gone. Strangely enough, there was little blood extant. What in heaven's name was this thing?

The Wraith had no time to delay. Even wounded, the creature was a formidable foe of uncanny strength. No matter what it was, or where it came from, this had to end now. The Wraith retrieved another flash pellet from his belt and aimed it at the heap's feet. Before the creature knew what was happening, the pellet had connected, sending its fiery energy upward, consuming the creature. With one last howl, it was gone, the only evidence of its existence a few ashes on the mossy ground.

The Wraith drew in several deep breaths, trying to regain his strength but also trying to make sense of the senseless. Was this creature another of Dr. Satanish's evil creations? He thought it likely, and cursed his arch-enemy's malevolence. But, the inevitability of reality soon set in and he knew he had to push forward. He hoped that, in time, he would find Leena and Max.

~ Chapter 7 ~

"**P**aul! Paul!" Leena cried out through the blackness of the forest. She strained her eyes as she tried to peer into the wet darkness surrounding her, desperately searching for the love of her life. A heavy hand dropped onto her shoulder and she gasped and wheeled.

"I'm sorry, Leena," Max said as she now recognized him. He raised his hands in apology. "I can barely see anything in this storm."

"It's all right," Leena said. "But where's Paul? I can't find him anywhere."

"I haven't seen him. I heard him cry out and then...nothing."

"Perhaps he fell down a ravine or in a trap or..."

"We'll find him," Max said, clearly trying to sound like a calming influence. "Let me try the comm-link." He did so. It was dead. Not a lack of a signal. Dead. Inactive. Inoperable. "I don't understand. Even if there was no signal, no contact with the chief, this thing should still be working. It's not even like the batteries are empty. It's just not working."

Leena tried to take in her surrounds, but she could see very little. "It's this place–Satan's Forest–it has to be."

With no way to locate Paul, and the darkness that surrounded was as intense as the raging storm, Leena and Max were forced to lock arms and shuffle their way through the brushy forest trail. Branches scratched at them as they pushed their way along.

The duo trudged for hours, making their way down the forest trail as it wound and twisted like a boa constrictor. The dirt path had long since turned to slick mud and both Leena and Max struggled to keep their footing as they plunged deeper and deeper into the heart of Satan's Forest. And whatever other mysteries lay there.

"Can you see anything?" Max shouted over the pouring rain and thunder.

"No," Leena shouted back. "But I think we're still on the path."

The day wore on. On and on they went, with no sight or sound of Paul. Leena was starting to really worry. Dusk was fast approaching.

"Should we keep going, or make camp?" Max's exhaustion-filled voice broke into her thoughts.

"Let's press on," Leena replied. "Try and find a clearing."

Max nodded and the linked duo continued onwards, their ponchos providing little protection from the torrential downpour. Branches seemingly attacked them from all sides. Max was tiring, Leena noticed, and it became harder going as she tried to push him forward while also struggling to maintain her own footing.

She felt Max's arm tug at hers before she heard his cry. He slipped, falling off the trail and into the brush, taking Leena with him. Max landed on the ground with a thump, Leena landing smack bang on top of him. They both grunted with the impact.

"Max? Are you all right?" she quickly asked while checking her own condition.

Max groaned as he slowly got to his feet and tried to wipe off the mud and grit on his hands on his wet pants. "I'll live. Sorry about that. Lost my footing on a loose rock."

"Let's get back on the trail and keep going," Leena said. "We need to find a clearing."

As they rejoined the path and made a few halting forward steps, a flash of lightning suddenly struck near them. The brilliant bolt of fire from the sky lit Max and Leena's position only for a moment, but that moment was enough for Leena to catch sight of something up ahead.

"Max," she said.

"What is it?"

Leena squinted, but in the darkness could see nothing further. But she was certain she had seen something.

"I'm not sure," Leena said. "I thought I saw something over there."

"What did you see? I can't see anything in this din."

"It was for a split-second, when the lightning struck. It was...a house?" Leena said, wondering if perhaps she was seeing things.

As if in reply, another bolt of lightning flashed through the darkening sky. Off in the distance, just visible through the trees, was what appeared to be a small house. An instant later, the house again vanished into the darkness.

"I saw it," Max said. "It *is* a house of some sort."

"If anything, it might provide us some shelter for the night."

They headed in the direction of the small abode as quickly as they could. It soon became apparent that it was a small log cabin, the kind Bob Ross often painted on television, albeit in dilapidated form. The wood was rotting in places and covered in a slimy, green moss. The windows were shattered, and vines snaked here and there throughout them. But the roof appeared solid so Leena and Max readily made their way inside, through the ramshackle door.

It was reasonably dry within, and the cabin was filled with dusty, rustic furniture. Crockery layed about on the dining table, and cabinets were open, filled with the trappings of a former life.

"Somebody used to live here," Leena said. "In the middle of nowhere."

"An old trapper's house, maybe," Max said as he sat in one of the dining chairs. It creaked under his weight but held firm.

There was a closed door to their left side, which Leena opened and shone her flashlight within. It was a tiny bedroom, with an open closet on one side, a shattered mirror on the other, and a dresser. She caught sight of a flintlock pistol that lay on the dresser. Leena approached it and picked it up. Closer inspection revealed the pistol was still loaded and she carefully lowered it back onto the dresser. She had no desire to get shot. She then noticed a faint carving, that of the initials E.B., on the pistol's barrel.

Setting the pistol aside momentarily, Max then joined her, took the pistol up, and did some exploring of his own. Turning away from the dresser, he swept his flashlight over the room one more time.

"What was that?" Leena said.

Max shone the light at the same place, into the open closet. Something metallic caused a glint to shine through. Max pushed aside dusty black overcoats hanging off a wooden rack. Hidden in the back of the closet was a rusted steel bookshelf upon which one book lay sentinel. He reached for it and grabbed the dusty, leather-bound tome.

Leena and Max took seats at the dining table and placed the thick book on the table before them.

"What do we have here?" Leena said, touching the book carefully.

It was bound in black leather, the cover embossed with gold print—although long since faded—it was still barely visible, and it read:

Journal of E. S. Branfeild
Witch Hunter
1710 –

Curiously, there was no end date. Leena opened the weathered journal and quickly flipped through the yellowed pages. It was only about three-quarters filled. The rest of the journal was blank, ink never having touched the pages.

"Fascinating," Leena murmured as she inspected the journal.

"What does it say?" Max said, peering over Leena's shoulder.

"Let's find out."

They went on to read together, and the journal went as follows:

It is the seventeenth day of February in the year of our Lord seventeen ten. My God-given name is Eliza Solomon Branfeild, and I was born into the role and profession I now pursue. And then, ten years ago, my talents were formally recognized, and I was appropriately appointed by my comrades in the Puritan movement into their Military Order of Witch Finders as a witch-finder and demon-router. I have carried out this glorious profession for over ten years now, traveling long and far to protect God's children from the tendrils of Satan and his wicked forces. In many of my travels I have encountered pirates, undead Haitians, and even persons possessing the blood-sucking qualities of bats. The longer I have traveled, the more certain I have become of the fragile position God's children have on this earth and how easy it is to be overrun by the forces of evil. This realization has only hardened my belief that good Puritan values are the only thing keeping the men and women of England, the Americas and the world from falling into death and despair. That, and comrades like myself within the order, who have been dispatched throughout the land to protect God-fearing men and women from all manner of Satan's creatures. I have most recently–

"Leena, I think you ought to see this," Max said.

Leena, so engrossed in the book's story, had failed to notice Max was now looking more closely around the cabin's living area.

"What have you found?"

She quickly joined him in the corner of what stood as the home's living room. Max was crouched there in the shadows. Before him, moldering in the dust and dirt, was a body. Black, tattered robes covering the skeletal remains. Beside the remains lay a tall black hat with a rusted buckle binding it together. Surprisingly, the hat was in far better condition than the clothing.

"I wonder if this was the resident?" Max asked, Leena crouching beside him to get a better view of the corpse.

"I'd say it was highly likely," Leena said. "Look at that outfit. It roughly matches the dates listed in the journal, I'd hazard a guess."

Upon closer view, they both noticed a small chain around the body's neck. Leena reached down and carefully removed it. It was a necklace. A small yellow gold disc with a cross imprinted on it. Under the cross were the initials E.B.

"We have our answer. This appears to have been Eliza Branfeild," Leena said.

"The journal," Max said, standing and looking back toward the table. "I wonder what happened to her."

"The journal may have some answers," Leena said. "It's worth checking out either way."

They returned to it. Leena sat and started flicking to the end of the book.

"You're flipping backwards?" Max said.

"I'm trying to find the last entry," Leena said. "We're more likely to find answers there than anywhere else."

Max nodded in agreement.

"Here we go." Leena had quickly found what she was looking for. She shone her flashlight down on the last entry in the journal, and she and Max began to read.

~ Chapter 8 ~

I *believe it is still the year of our Lord seventeen hundred and ten, or perhaps it is later...my mind is befuddled. I fear that my end is near at hand. I am so weary I find myself barely able to hold pen to paper, but I know I must. I write what I do now so that future intruders into the woodlands known as Satan's Forest may be saved from a fate akin to that of my colleagues and my own. If you read this journal, heed my warning!*

ESCAPE FROM SATAN'S FOREST WHILE YOU STILL CAN!

All who enter, or remain here for too long, are damned to a ring of hell so cruel that Dante dare not write of it. But I shall, if only to prevent others from falling into this pit of damnation.

THIS FOREST IS A PLACE OF MADNESS!

I do not know how long ago my comrades and I entered the forest. I do not even know the current date. All I know is that my comrades and I entered the woods that have gained the foreboding name of Satan's Forest on the third day of November in the year of our Lord seventeen hundred and ten.

We were summoned to the forest by a desperate letter from the mayor of the neighboring village of Bidbury. The mayor begged us to investigate the haunted forest that borders their town after a multitude of his townsfolk had ventured into the forest, never to return.

Having just concluded a case where we routed a nest of bat-like creatures, our group set out at once for Bidbury. Once we arrived, the mayor and townsfolk fully explained their dastardly situation to us as follows:

The town of Bidbury was founded in 1595, nestled cozily within the forest, and was home to a hundred English and Welsh immigrants. The colony flourished initially, growing from a village to a small town.

But one hundred years after it was first settled, a sudden darkness fell upon Bidbury. The weather turned dark and moody, crops began to fail, babies began to die, and sickness became rampant. The town council became convinced these troubles were caused by a witch, or a number of witches, within the town's midst, and that the casting of spells and performance of black magic were the source of the town's woes. And so, the town conducted an investigation and seven women were burned at the stake on suspicion of being a witch. One woman who was burned was of particular note–as she burned, she laughed hysterically at the townsfolk, cursed them and the forest surrounding them, and she pledged herself to darkness eternally if it would allow her to endure in the woods. After this incident, the town's troubles subsided. For a time.

But then the troubles re-ignited with a fury akin to that of hell itself. Buildings were set ablaze, the village was wracked with disease, and townsfolk disappeared into the trees that surrounded the town. And everyone, without fail, reported hearing a strange, evil voice calling them deeper into the woods. There were reported sightings of a strange, shadowy woman who bore a haunting resemblance to the mad, hysterical woman they had burned at the stake.

When the townsfolk could no longer endure this pestilence, they fled their homes and re-established a new town of Bidbury outside of the woods. The cabins and buildings that once made up the original town of Bidbury were left to the forest and whatever dark forces inhabited it.

The establishment of the new town of Bidbury proved exceedingly difficult as the townsfolk now had less manpower and resources, having abandoned their original homes and much of their worldly possessions. However, with much effort, the new town was firmly established, and once again, began to thrive in its own small way. From that moment forward, the woods were off-limits to the townsfolk. The legend of Satan's Forest was now, in their eyes, fact.

Things did not remain calm for long. Whatever evil possessed the forest was not yet done with the people of Bidbury. Many men within the town inexplicably were drawn into the woods, never to be seen or heard from again. Others recounted they could hear the siren call of one who was irresistible. Only when forcibly held back, or placed in shackles, were they able to resist the call into the woods. The townsfolk were baffled and terrified by these horrific occurrences, and that is why I, Eliza Solomon Branfeild and my team from the Puritan's Military Order of Witch Finders, were called to Bidbury to investigate the supernatural happenings occurring there.

My team, including myself, comprised of four members, and they were as follows:

Eliza Solomon Branfeild, leader. I was chosen for this role in part due to my special powers. I am a direct descendent of one of the world's preeminent witch-hunters and I have the unique ability to connect with, and rout, witches and similar supernatural creatures. These powers and abilities were passed down to me through the bloodline of my maternal grandmother, Eliza Solomon, world-renowned witch-hunter in her lifetime.

Robert Charles Elsworth, our experienced weapons and navigation expert.

Howard Abram Singleton, our resident occult expert with missionary experience across the globe.

Jackson Laurence Pierce, a witchfinder-in-training assigned to our group by the Witchfinder General.

We gathered supplies and entered the woods on the third day in November in the year of our Lord seventeen hundred and ten. Almost immediately we found ourselves disoriented and lost within Satan's Forest. From there, our venture went steadily, and horrifyingly, downhill. We quickly realized these woods are truly host to an enchantress who controls this forest with demonic certainty. I believe it to be the woman the townsfolk told us who laughed hysterically as she burned at the stake.

We had barely begun our task when Singleton tripped over an unseen root, tumbled down a hill and broke his neck on a large boulder. We took the time to give him a proper Christian burial before moving on, but we were already shaken to our cores before we had achieved anything.

Within what felt like a day we reached the former town of Bidbury, only to find it had been completely overrun by the expanding forest, reclaiming the town as its own. It was an eerie sight, one which certainly set us all on edge.

Elsworth, Pierce, and I holed up in an abandoned cabin where we attempted to conduct rituals to give us strength and began to make plans for our next steps.

On our second night there, Pierce vanished from the cabin in the middle of the night. Whether he left the abode of his own accord, or was taken from us by some unseen force, we saw or heard nothing. In the morning, however, we were horrified to discover his naked corpse hanging from a nearby tree. The noose comprised of vines that littered the forest in abundance. Elsworth suggested he had committed suicide, but I found such a suggestion to be absurd. What reason could there be? But, as long as doubt remained, we could not conduct a proper Christian burial.

A mere few days into our mission, our team had been reduced by half. I can only estimate at the amount of time we have been here, but those days had, in truth, felt like weeks, perhaps even months. Sunrise and sunset cannot be seen. The forest is so thick in this area, we are plunged into perpetual darkness. We try and sleep where and when we can, but rest is fitful and our dreams disturbing.

Elsworth and I chose to carry on, our mission incomplete. We set out into the woods, knowing not where we were headed, but prayed we would find the answers we were searching for and banish the evil amongst us. Another day or two later–who can say with any clarity?–we were shocked to find both Singleton and Pierce alive and well, treading the path up ahead toward us. They greeted us warmly and casually, neither wishing to talk about the fates that had obviously befallen them.

We were soon to discover they were not Singleton and Pierce. Upon constant questioning from Elsworth, the two lashed out, attacking us, and revealing their true forms. They appeared to be creatures of bark and leaf. As we fought, they would switch back and forth from creature to human. Their soulless eyes burned into ours as we struggled for our very lives. Ultimately, Elsworth and I dealt them fatal blows with the bolas Elsworth had provided us all with. The battle had taken its toll on Elsworth, however. His arm was badly mangled and his mind could not deal with the horrors we had thus far endured. I attempted to reach him, but he just stared off into the forest, his face a mixture of trepidation and repudiation. He would be of no further use to me.

Elsworth could walk but do nothing more, so we continued deeper into the forest, knowing not what we might yet befall. As we continued, many other incidents occurred, too horrifying to write of and I fear I have little time remaining for that. At last we did indeed find that which we had long sought: A creature so heinous, so foul as to defy the very laws of Heaven and Earth. She is a creature from Hell itself.

She is known merely as the Swamp Witch, residing within the vast swamp at the very depths of the aptly named Satan's Forest. All who enter here are damned to Satan's eternal domain. The Witch shall see to that. She makes use of her nefarious infernal powers to torment and kill all who enter it.

It was she who was responsible for everything within the forest, for all the disasters affecting my team, for the horrors infecting the village of Bidbury. She is Satan's ready servant, a collector of souls in his name, ready to do his bidding and cause harm to all and sundry. Like her creatures, she is a shape-shifter, with powers so malevolent, so powerful, as to be almost unstoppable. Perhaps she cannot be vanquished.

Elsworth and our company tried our best, but our weapons were useless and our incantations meaningless. It was as though God had forsaken us in our moment of need. We were powerless to do a thing. All we could do was attempt escape, flee with our lives, and hope we could, somehow, be free of the sinister confines of Satan's Forest. As we attempted our flight, Elsworth was lost. I know not what occurred, but he was gone, and I knew the Swamp Witch had somehow claimed him.

I was able to return to the cabin and have sought refuge here. Provisions are gone, and my sole remaining weapon–my trustworthy flintlock–is of no use against such an adversary. I am exhausted and alone. All hope is lost. I can hear the Swamp Witch's voice with every howl of the wind, with every crack of a tree branch, with every step across the muddy ground. Even when I sleep, she enters my dreams and wreaks havoc on my subconscious. It is through my dreams she has revealed to me her powers over this forest and anyone who enters. It is through my dreams she has promised me I will never leave alive.

I know she is right.

I write this journal in the hopes that perhaps it is one day found, and then that poor soul can flee in terror before entering the depths of this befouled place. I pray to God they may make their way to safety where I, and my colleagues, could not. The power here is too great for any human, even one as gifted as I, to counter.

I must end this journal now. I hear a disturbance outside the cabin. I still have my trusted flintlock pistol with one shot left in it. Whether I will use it on myself or my attacker, only God knows.

Godspeed and good luck to whoever finds this journal.
God's Faithful Servant

ELIZA SOLOMON BRANFEILD

~ Chapter 9 ~

Leena and Max finished reading Eliza Branfeild's last recorded words but could not stop staring at the page. At last, Leena closed the book and took a deep breath. "What a story."

"You can't...believe all that, surely," Max said.

"You know me. Ordinarily, I would be as disbelieving as you, but with what we've recently encountered–Aztekoth, the horrors of nature inflicted upon us by Dr. Satanish–I cannot just file this away as the words of some crazed, superstitious woman from the Dark Ages."

A feeling of dread suddenly flooded Leena's soul, and she knew they must leave, find Paul and be away from this place.

"You're right. And it does explain why the chief was drawn to this place." He rubbed at his jaw for a moment. "We can't stay here," Max said, as though he had read her mind.

"The storm is still active but seems to be lessening a little. Either way, I'd rather be out there looking for Paul than staying here and doing nothing."

Gathering their gear, they exited the cabin and started to re-trace their steps back toward the path into the forest. Once they had found the path, they slowly trudged along, their flashlights guiding their way. Leena felt the adrenaline of the situation fueling her every step. They had to find Paul. They just had to.

They continued on. The din of the storm, and of the forest itself, caused the hair on Leena's neck to stand on end, but onwards they pressed. She and Max cried Paul's name, hoping against hope he would somehow hear them and appear from the bushes alive and well.

A noise on the path ahead startled them. A rustling of leaves, a twisting of branches. They stopped and waited, listening. Leena tensed her muscles, her hands curling into fists. She was as ready as she could possibly be for a fight.

Paul emerged from the brush up ahead. He was disheveled and was trying to tidy himself up when Leena and Max approached him.

"Darling," Leena cried, rushing forward and embracing her fiancé. "We were so worried about you."

"So was I," Paul said. "You'll never believe what I saw in the forest."

"We've found a few things as well, Chief," Max said.

"Good, good," Paul said, his face beaming with joy. "I need to show you what I found. It's this way. Come with me."

Paul was plainly eager to get away, practically trying to drag Leena and Max with him. Leena was having none of it.

"What's wrong, Paul?" she said, breaking free from his grip. "This doesn't sound like you."

"I am Paul Sanderson," Paul said. He may have looked like Paul, but it was fast becoming obvious to Leena this was not her love at all. "Come, see what I've found."

"Leena," Max cried out. "That isn't Paul. It's one of those...creatures."

"Darling," Paul said with some sternness, "I need you to come with me, now. I need to show you."

Leena took a step back, away from the creature seeming to be masquerading as Paul. Max took a step forward to stand alongside her. Paul smiled and transformed before their eyes. While its face remained a version of Paul's, though now extended and distorted, its body was thin and skeletal, with bark-like skin covering its body from its stony hooves up to its stringy, moss-like hair flopping down over an eerie version of Paul's face.

"What the..." Max could only say.

"What are you? Where is Paul?" Leena demanded.

The creature merely hissed in anger, not moving from its vantage point at the brushy edge of the path.

"Leena, let's back away...carefully..." Max said softly, in a clear effort to not to agitate the creature any further.

Leena acquiesced, the two retreating slowly, step by step. The creature watched them carefully then emitted a deathly hiss and launched itself at them. Max took the brunt of the attack, the creature pummeling into him and letting fly with blows from its wooden appendages. Max grunted in pain; they rolled in the earth, wrestling, struggling for their lives. Leena took the opportunity to pounce, grabbed the creature by an arm, yanked it up and flung it over her shoulder in an expertly-maneuvered judo throw. The creature crashed into the adjacent foliage, shrieking as it hit brush and dirt.

But it wasn't defeated. It immediately jumped back to its feet and charged back into the fray. It was faster this time, and Leena barely had time to side-step as it swiped at her with its right arm. Unfortunately, she wasn't quite fast enough to avoid the spiky wooden claws of the creature embedding into her arm, drawing blood. Leena let out a cry and kicked the creature in the stomach, knocking it backwards.

She immediately grabbed hold of her injured arm, putting pressure on the wound. Blood oozed from in between her fingers. She grimaced in pain and hoped there were no splinters.

The creature again, but now she was ready. It lashed out with both arms, ready to attack, to kill. She nimbly side-stepped it and, as the creature rushed past, she reached out and grabbed it by its head and neck and gave a mighty twist. A mighty crack, as though a tree had been toppled by a lumberjack, and the creature fell to the ground in a heap. Leena stumbled back, took a deep breath, and hoped that was the end of it.

It wasn't.

The creature jumped to its feet again, its head lolling to one side, its sinister Paul-like visage smiling lasciviously.

"Oh no," Leena said as her arm throbbed and her muscles ached.

"This thing is unbeatable," Max said.

"No," Leena muttered, "nothing is unbeatable. I refuse to accept that."

The creature advanced toward them, hissing, promising them nothing but pain and misery. Leena knew it had to end now. She reached into her backpack and removed some pellets from an interior pocket. She held them aloft.

"Flash pellets," Max cried.

They were indeed. Leena lobbed them at the foot of the creature. They exploded there in a fiery inferno. The creature shrieked in eternal agony as the conflagration spread upwards, totally consuming the creature from the worst of nightmares. In moments, the shrieking stopped, and the creature was gone, vanquished.

Max moved over to Leena, saw her injured arm and held it up to get a better look at it. "It's not too bad a wound, nothing deep, no ligament damage." He removed his backpack and retrieved a bandage from within. "This will stop the bleeding."

"Thank you, Max."

After a few moments to catch their breath, they began to try and take stock of their situation.

"So," Max started, "the journal was right. Shape-shifting creatures, swamp witches. What have we gotten ourselves into, here?"

"This place is a nightmare," Leena said. "We have to find Paul and get out of here as quickly as possible."

"You're right," Max said, "but this place...what do we do about Satan's Forest?"

Leena shivered. She didn't know how to answer that.

*　*　*　*　*　*

Deep in Satan's Forest, deeper than anyone had dared venture for a millennia, something moved. Something was displeased. It had failed to capture or kill the invaders of its domain.

"Very well," the Swamp Witch said. "They have brought this upon themselves. I will strike and their souls will burn in damnation for their defiance of me."

She cackled at that, a deep, terrible howl that echoed out from her vantage point, through the swamps and forest, into the very souls of...

* * * * * *

"Did you hear that, Max?" Leena whispered.

"What was it?" Max said. "The wind?"

"I don't know," she replied, "but I could have sworn it was...laughing."

~ Chapter 10 ~

The Wraith trudged through the muddy waters that pooled under the trees in this part of Satan's Forest. In time, the swamp began to drain away, forming a trickling, shallow stream The Wraith continued through with little difficulty. On either side of the stream, the land was thick with brush and trees, and The Wraith thought it best to continue his way through the water toward...

I need to find Leena and Max. This place is so vast, so treacherous, and my tracking systems are inoperable...I don't know how to best proceed.

Onwards he marched; the stream began to widen and deepen into a full-fledged river, and he was soon forced to make his way ashore. The brush was a little thinner at this point, but not by much, and his journey slowed, his way forward often blocked by thick brush and gigantic tree roots. He managed to continue alongside the now-surging river.

After a long trek which, in truth, wasn't great in distance, The Wraith stopped for a moment. He gazed out over the river which shone a bright green tinge through his night-vision lenses, and wondered.

I don't recall seeing a river this size on the map. I'm sure I'm still within Satan's Forest, but...

The pause in activity caused his arm and ribs to throb, or at least took his mind off the job at hand, which reminded him of the constant dull ache within his body. He quickly shrugged it off. He needed to be mentally alert for whatever this place would undoubtedly throw at him. And he had to find his friends. It was now more important than ever.

"Paul..."

He heard the voice behind him and whirled, fists cocked, ready to fight. But there was no one there. He scanned the area with his night-vision lenses, but saw nothing.

That voice again, Paul thought. *Calling to me, beckoning me.*

He turned back toward the river's edge and started his way alongside its path once again.

"Paul...come to me, Paul..."

The woman's voice seemed to come at him from all directions, seemingly from nowhere but everywhere all at once. He couldn't explain it. He also couldn't explain why he was so drawn to it. His muscles tensed. He knew he mustn't answer the call, but somehow he had to.

He had to.

"Come to me, Paul..."

Frustrated, he cried out, "Who are you? What do you want from me?"

Silence followed his outburst and The Wraith breathed deeply, trying to collect himself. Slowly he lowered and unclenched his fists then massaged his bad arm.

"Come to me, Paul. I need you."

The Wraith found the urge to move irresistible. He had to go, to be with her, to answer her siren call.

No!

The mental exertion was intense, but he fought the desire to move into the forest. His body shook, his muscles pounded, but he held firm. With great difficulty, he turned and forced himself back down toward the river. Perhaps he could enter the water, swim to the other side, get away from the voice.

Perhaps.

He plunged into the raging depths and began to swim. He quickly realized the mistake he had made. The current was powerful here, almost white water in its intensity, and his strength was weakening. The voice had clouded his judgment, and now he was being swept downriver at building speed, unable to break free of its powerful grip.

The Wraith found it challenging to keep his head above water such was the ferocity of the raging, white waves enveloping him. It was all he could do to stay afloat, catching slight gasps of air, as the current bore him away.

Then he saw it.

At first he thought it was a log or branch, some piece of flotsam being drawn down the river alongside him, but then it shifted in the water and The Wraith realized it wasn't floating at all. It was swimming. And it was moving towards him. Two strobing, yellow eyes and a leathery snout cut their way through the dark water directly for him. They were massive. The Wraith knew the true extent of the alligator lay beneath the surface of the water–the rows of sharp teeth, clawed feet and a powerful tail all remained hidden below the surface as the gator steadily approached him. The fact there should be no alligators in this part of the world meant nothing at that moment. Here it was, and here it had to be dealt with.

The Wraith felt a chill run down his body. He was helpless to fight the raging torrent; even staying afloat was becoming too much to handle, and now this. The gator grew closer to him. Its eyes were locked onto him with a reptilian hunger.

Closer and closer.

Then it pounced, splashing up and out of the river, intending The Wraith to be its next meal.

It lunged at him, its jaws open wide to reveal rows of jagged, glistening teeth. The Wraith barely had time to extend his arms out but managed to do so, grabbing the creature's massive jaws before its teeth could slice into him. The gator snapped at him, but The Wraith, using all the strength he could muster, held firm, preventing the monster from making contact with its mighty teeth. They thrashed about in a titanic struggle over life and death. The alligator attempted a death roll, trying to pummel The Wraith beneath the water, to drown him, but the Dread Avenger was having none of it. He managed to leap up and onto the creature's back, away from its deadly jaws, and held on for dear life.

The alligator continued to thrash about, trying to shake its oppressor loose, but The Wraith held his grip. His right arm was on fire and his ribs felt like they were turning to mush. He knew something would soon give, and he doubted it would be the creature beneath him.

He still had a chance. Just before his right arm gave out, The Wraith let go of the creature and dove back into the murky depths. The giant reptile turned its head sideways, tried grabbing at The Wraith with its powerful jaws, but ultimately bit into nothing but air.

With the quickness of a man desperate to survive, The Wraith grabbed hold of the gator's jaws once again and wrapped his good arm around them, stopping the gator from opening its mouth. Then, despite the rushing water pushing both him and the thrashing gator downstream, he reached around for his cape with his injured free arm and detached it from his back. While holding the gator's mouth shut with one arm, The Wraith proceeded to loop his cape around the gator's jaws with the other, wrapping it tightly around and tying it into a knot. He hoped it would hold. The alligator struggled valiantly, but The Wraith's bulletproof cape held firm.

It thrashed about, flailing out with its mighty tail, almost catching The Wraith a deadly blow, but he somehow managed to keep out of the creature's reach. The current was unbelievably strong here, and it gave The Wraith an idea. Quickly, he ducked under the water, underneath the gator, and reached out, giving it a powerful shove with his remaining strength. He reached the surface and saw what he had prayed for–the gator was being swept down river away from him.

He was safe.

It was only once the alligator was swept out of sight that The Wraith took a moment to breathe. He barely had strength to tread water, but somehow he had to make his way ashore, to break free from this river prison. With an almighty surge, he managed to extricate himself from the center of the current into weaker waters off to the side, and from there, was able to weakly paddle to shore. He clutched at dirt and weed, dragged himself up out of the water. He lay there, not able to move another inch. He gasped for air, allowed his lungs to fill with oxygen and his limbs to relax. His mind was awhirl, exhaustion set in, darkness beckoning. He let his eyes close.

"Paul!"

His eyes snapped open. He knew that voice. Could it be she had found him? That they're safe?

"Chief, are you okay?" Max cried out.

The Wraith, a sodden, muddy mess, sat upright, and caught sight of both Leena and Max standing before him. Leena crouched down and took him in her arms.

"Darling, where have you been? We've been searching everywhere for you."

Then, a troubled look came over her and she stood, taking a step back. The Wraith didn't know what to make of this.

"It...is you, Paul, isn't it?" she said.

The Wraith struggled to his feet, confused. "Of course it is. Who do you think I am?"

Leena embraced him once again. "You wouldn't believe what Max and I have been through."

The Wraith smiled and removed his cowl. "I have a few stories for you both, as well." He turned and gazed back out over the river. "Tell me, Max, what do you think of alligators?"

Max raised an eyebrow, clearly bewildered by the question. "Not too much. The further I am from them, the better."

Paul smiled. "Then we better get away from this river as fast as we can."

"What?" Max said.

~ Chapter 11 ~

"**A**nd I had finally managed to get ashore when you two found me." The Wraith finished his extraordinary tale. Leena and Max remained silent, evidently taking it all in. A short time ago, Leena and Max had done likewise, recounting their exploits over the last couple days or so, detailing their encounters with shape-shifting creatures and their discovery of Eliza Branfeild and her amazing journal. And the apparent existence of a Swamp Witch deep within the belly of Satan's Forest.

Days? Was it only a few days? Or was it weeks? He grappled with this conundrum for a few moments, but he honestly could not tell just how long they had been there. It was this place, Satan's Forest. It had some sort of...supernatural...hold over all who entered it. Time became an ethereal, immutable thing, seeming both unchanging and never-ending at the same time. Their equipment proved useless, and even their watches–The Wraith's new Héron Marinor, Leena's Rolex, and Max's antique Longines pocket watch–had ceased working, unable to be wound back into operation.

As they spoke and pondered the menacing situation, they decided to head to what they determined was the very heart of Satan's Forest. Whatever–whomever–was responsible for the sinister goings on, they would find it there. The Wraith was determined to find the answers, and vanquish the evil within.

It was now day, or at least The Wraith estimated it to be, but the sky was dark and ominous as though a storm was brewing, but there was no rain. No visible sun nor moon nor stars. It was impossible to tell the time by any recognizable measure. However, as he currently did not need his night-vision lenses, nor Leena and Max their flashlights, The Wraith felt sure it was day. So was the sense of his internal biological clock, anyway.

"I don't know," Leena said as they continued their journey, "I feel certain it's only been two days or so since we entered this land."

"Could be longer," Max said without offering any reason why.

The Wraith removed a glove, rubbed his chin, felt the stubble there. "I'd say at least three days, give or take, based on my beard growth. It's impossible to say for sure. Time seems to have little meaning here."

Max shrugged, felt his own stubble, and the trio pressed on, marching toward their destiny. Onwards they went, keeping silent vigil over each other, determined to make good progress. The path in this section of the forest was clearer, smoother, and despite their predicament and the thought of what lay ahead, The Wraith felt a renewed strength and purpose. No matter what evil they may encounter, they would tackle it as they always had–together.

Their travails continued for hours, as best The Wraith could estimate, all keeping silent, all remaining steadfast in their resolve.

After what felt an eternity more, Max finally broke the silence. "And so we penetrated deeper and deeper into the heart of darkness."

Leena arched an eyebrow at Max's choice of quote. "Conrad, Max? I didn't realize you were so well-read."

"I'm not just a pretty face, you know," Max said. "I don't just read scientific or electronic journals."

"My apologies," Leena said in a jestful tone. "I should have known better."

The Wraith gave Max a tight smile, but his mind was elsewhere. Max's quoting of Conrad reminded him of another classical work: Macbeth by Shakespeare. He had first read it at school–or at least the original Paul Sanderson had– as most students do, but coming from such a troubled family, the tragic horror in the play had affected him to the point where he no longer sought out the play. Within its pages there were three supernatural creatures that had unnerved him greatly as a child of unloving, inattentive parents, to a point where he tried not to think of them. But once the mind tries not to think of something, that thing becomes the only thing one's mind can think of. Even the Michael Reeve side of him could not force these feelings aside.

In the back of The Wraith's mind he heard a seductive voice utter a simple sentence, but one that made the hairs on his arms stand up.

"By the pricking of my thumbs, something wicked this way comes."

He heard those words over and over again. He shivered and without realizing, rubbed the back of his head with a gloved hand.

"Hey!" Max's voice shook him from his reverie. "There's a clearing up ahead."

The Wraith and Leena pushed forward to join their friend in what was exactly as Max had said–a large clearing. Before them lay an expanse of grass–strangely short and well-kept–with a small pond off to the right side. Surrounding the clearing were massive trees that all stood less than a foot apart, creating an ominous ring encircling them. It was as though they had somehow become imprisoned by an impenetrable, wooden barrier.

"This is...interesting," Leena said, taking in her surroundings.

The Wraith walked past her, crouched down, felt the lawn with his hands. "This looks freshly mowed, and yet...isn't. It doesn't make any sense."

"Nothing in this place does, Chief," Max said.

The Wraith plopped down onto the soft grass, and Leena and Max quickly joined him. There was no way of knowing for sure, but The Wraith felt certain they were not yet where they needed to be. He removed his cowl and wiped his brow.

"I could use a bit of a breather," Leena said, laying down in the comfortable turf. Paul caught sight of her gazing into the sky; he followed her view. The sky was still murky, gloomy, with nothing to discern it as actual sky. No clouds or sun or any sign of life.

Leena turned her head to the side to look at Paul. He looked back. No matter what wickedness awaited them, they were together, and that was all that mattered. He saw Leena felt the same way.

Thankfully, the siren voice was no longer in evidence, but he knew it could return at any moment. He had to be ready. *They* had to be ready. "Leena, Max," Paul started. "If...that voice returns, if I hear its call once more, you must do all you can to restrain me. I'm not sure I can resist it again, especially if we are actually nearing its source."

Leena sat upright, concern etched into her beautiful features. "We promise, Paul. We won't let them take you." She smiled weakly, but Paul knew there was fear behind that smile. In truth, he felt it as well. He was brave, strong, but only a fool held no fear. And he was no fool.

He returned his sight to the sky, still perplexed by its mysterious appearance. The darkness of it all began to lull him into a relaxing stupor, sleep beckoning to him once again, when he noticed a thin mist emerging from the surrounding trees. The sight of it, the unnaturalness of it, the growing intensity of it floating in waves toward them, jostled Paul back to his senses, and the three of them stood quickly.

"What...what is it?" Leena said, fear clearly evident in her voice.

"It looks like a mist," Max said, "but this can't be any true mist."

"Stand back," Paul said as he quickly placed his cowl over his head. "Head back the way we came, for those trees there." He pointed the way.

They started in that direction, but the mist was soon upon them, quicker than they anticipated. The Wraith felt an overwhelming urge to sleep, to rest. It was too much, he couldn't take it, hadn't the strength to resist. He saw Leena and Max buckling as well.

I have to get away...Leena...Max...

Darkness.

＊　＊　＊　＊　＊

Leena awoke with a start and sat up immediately. She had no idea how long she had been out. The mist had vanished but the clearing was now bathed in a strange, even darker hue. It was a blackness not of the night, but of an atmosphere science and common sense could not comprehend. It was hard to even see her hand before her face.

"Paul?" she called. "Where are you?" She turned left and right, heard no sign of him and could see very little on top of that. "Paul?" she said again.

Still nothing.

She walked carefully, trying to make out where she remembered seeing Paul last. No matter where she stood, there was no sign of him.

"Max? Are you there? Paul's gone missing again." There was no word from the Irishman either.

Fear and trepidation began to overwhelm her and she started to shake. It was happening again, but this time she was alone. And the Swamp Witch and her monstrous creatures were out there, somewhere, possibly nearby. The thought was almost too unbearable to cope with.

She stumbled about in a mad attempt to find them both, but all she managed to do was lose her footing and she slipped into the pond with a loud splash. She sputtered and hacked the water from her lungs, crawling her way through the mud back onto solid ground. She cursed her fearfulness, knew she had betrayed Paul's teachings.

This place was beginning to affect her.

"Paul! Max!" she shouted. Again, no reply came.

She stood, tried to make sense of her predicament, tried to plan for what her next step might be. She turned, searching as best she could at her surrounds, but visibility was still poor and she could see or hear nothing. An eerie silence was all that greeted her; she could not help but shiver once more.

She remained at the pond's edge, not knowing what to do or where to go. She had to do something but, for the life of her, her mind was blank. She had no idea what her next course of action should be. As confused as she was, she realized again the forest, or some malicious force within, was affecting her and her judgment.

And it was worsening.

She tried to calm herself, took a few deep breaths. Let the air flow, let the mind clear, let the nerves settle. It was beginning to work, and she slowly started feeling more herself again. Visibility remained poor but she tried to look about her once more. Behind her was the pond, its water still and clear. She found herself looking down into it, saw her reflection and, strangely, couldn't take her eyes off the mirrored image. She crouched down to get a better view. The sight was as clear as a mirror, not like water at all. How strange, how...captivating. Then, her reflection smiled at her. Leena gasped. The reflection laughed then pointed off to its left. Leena couldn't help but look in that direction, and let out a horrified shriek. There, under the water, merely inches below the surface, lay The Wraith and Max, their hands crossed over their chests, their skin a pale and sickly blue. Dead.

"No!" Leena screamed. She rushed into the water, determined to save them both. They were not dead, they couldn't be. She had to save them, she just had to.

When she had reached the spot where they lay, she plunged her hands into the water, flailed about there, groping amongst the sandy dirt of the pond floor. But there was no sign of them. She continued on. They must be there; she had seen them with her very own eyes.

Then she stopped. *No*, she thought. This was another of the Swamp Witch's tricks. She had to pull herself together, not let herself be swayed by illusory tricks. Whatever had happened to Paul and Max, she would be of no use to them if she fell apart now.

She stepped out of the pond again. She was saturated, but cared little for that under the circumstances. The safety of Paul and Max was paramount, and she knew she had to leave the clearing and try and find the Swamp Witch's hidden lair.

With some difficulty, she located her backpack, pulled it over her shoulders and started to make her way for the surrounding trees. She had but moved a few steps when she was startled by a noise behind her, coming from the pond. She was glued to her position, unable to move. Whether through fear or some external force, she knew not. The sound started as a light rippling of liquid, which grew into an intense bubbling and boiling as though a volcanic eruption was being spewed from the very pond.

Leena couldn't move, couldn't even turn her head, such was the force binding her to the spot. Sweat beaded her brow, but she could not wipe it away—could barely think—when an icy hand gripped her shoulders. Suddenly, she was free to move, and she swiveled, catching sight of black and decaying fingers.

"Hello, Leena. I've been expecting you."

In the next instant that she was conscious, Leena knew this was the Swamp Witch, knew she was in trouble, but darkness was looming.

She never had a chance to scream.

~ Chapter 12 ~

The Wraith awoke slowly, as if from a dream that had shades of reality in it. Then he fully opened his eyes and took in the living, breathing nightmare he was fully immersed in.

He tried to get up and move but found himself unable to. He gasped as he realized his arms and legs were bound, not by coarse ropes, but by hundreds of small vines twisted together to form bigger vines that made movement of any kind impossible.

The Wraith turned his head to the side to see what it was he had been bound to. To his shock, he found himself bound to a tall tree, his arms tied to the higher branches while his feet were bound to the trunk. And try as he might, he found himself unable to move not even an inch. The more he struggled, the more he pulled against the vines and the tighter they encircled his limbs, digging into his suit. He ground his teeth together in a mix of pain and frustration.

He was completely immobilized, effectively tied to the tree. Tied to the wood. The horror of his nightmare soon after entering Satan's Forest had been brought to perverse life.

"Chief?" The Wraith whipped his head around to seek out the source of Max's voice. His friend was in a similar predicament, imprisoned to his right.

"Where are we?" Max asked.

The Wraith shook his head then looked away from his friend. The horror of their situation and surroundings were brought home to him then.

The Wraith and Max were trapped in a swamp. The two trees they were bound to were part of a sinister ring of rotted and twisted trees that surrounded a murky pool of water. One massive tree in the ring particularly caught The Wraith's attention. It seemed to be three smaller trees whose roots had grown entangled and the trees themselves had somehow merged into one, creating one wooden testament to the perversion of nature that was Satan's Forest. On the opposite side of the ring appeared to be a small cave. The entrance to the cave was obscured in shadow, but an awful gurgling sound emanated from deep within. A muddy stream snaked its way from the cave, feeding the pool with liquid.

Various, hideous pieces of flotsam bobbed and swayed within the pool. The Wraith noted it was filled with body parts in various forms of decay, the pool resembling that of a foul, monstrous cauldron filled with soup.

The soup of the dead.

The Wraith realized they had reached their destination. This was the lair of the Swamp Witch of Satan's Forest.

The sight of the pool before him darkened The Wraith's soul. Such depravity, such malevolence. He knew not how they would escape, but escape they must or all was lost.

He turned to face Max once again. His friend had paled considerably, no doubt realizing what the pool contained. Even The Wraith felt the struggle to remain composed.

"What is this place?" Max said at last rather pointlessly.

"We are where we intended to be, and where we were intended to be. Clearly we've been brought here but for what reason I cannot yet say."

"The mist," Max said. "It enveloped us and...that's the last thing I remember."

The Wraith said nothing, but his experience was the same. The reality of their situation dawned on him. The Swamp Witch had been toying with them. They had been but pawns in her Machiavellian schemes, nothing they had done had proven to have an effect on the outcome whatsoever. Such power. Such evil. The Wraith worried it was beyond their ken to combat. But Leena...where was Leena?

He turned his face left and right as best he could. He called out her name, but there came no reply. As best he could determine, Leena was not imprisoned with them. Her whereabouts were a mystery.

"Maybe she was able to escape," Max said, perhaps hoping against hope. "She was a little ways to the side when the mist hit us."

The Wraith could nothing more than hope Max was right, that Leena had indeed escaped and was still safe somewhere out there in Satan's Forest.

Safe, he thought. *The word has no meaning here. No one here can be safe at this...monster's whim.*

He fought once again to free himself from his binds, but it was no good. The vines were like steel. There was no purchase there, and his strength was waning. Here they were imprisoned–crucified in a way–and here they would remain.

That was the Swamp Witch's plan all along, The Wraith felt sure.

The pool suddenly came to life with a boiling rage, bubbles roiling to the surface as though it was a pot placed on a boiling stove. The water began to erupt in a fiery inferno akin to Dante's Hell and, at the center of the pool, a shape arose from the depths.

Her skin was the color of rotted flesh. She wore what appeared to be a torn, dark dress, but was not merely rags. Her skin, or what passed as such, was covered with insects and fungi. Her hideous teeth were yellow and blackened in places, rotting away as was everything else on her person. Maggots spewed from her lips, and what hair she had left was grey and stringy, twisted beyond beauty by the corruption of time. She had eyes so dark they were not black. They were twin voids, two pits, two absences of light through which she regarded her hellish domain.

The Wraith glared into the witch's eyes, into its soul, and was sickened by what he saw and felt. It was as though he was staring into the very depths of Hell itself.

The Swamp Witch stepped forth from the gurgling pool and stood before The Wraith in all of her desecrated glory. There was nothing human left there, The Wraith determined, only pure, unadulterated evil. Her soul was condemned. Satan had bequeathed her this and more.

"Hello...Paul..." she rasped, her voice an indescribable, grotesque tone. The Swamp Witch smiled at The Wraith through her disgusting lips and licked them lasciviously with a maggot-ridden tongue. He couldn't help but gag at the sight and smell of her.

"What are you?" The Wraith said through gritted teeth. "What do you want from us?"

"Oh, I think you know who I am," the Swamp Witch replied in a somewhat jestful tone, drawing closer to him, causing his gag reflex to run wild again. "And I think you know what I want."

"My soul," The Wraith hacked. "My eternal soul."

"Very good," the witch cackled. "My master beckons me to do his bidding. It is souls he craves, and souls I have given him for centuries and more." Her face contorted in a mixture of anger and frustration, though it was honestly hard for The Wraith to tell. "This forest here is my domain, but it is also my prison. I was condemned here, burned at the stake here, and here I must remain, my master's ever-eager servant."

The Wraith's surmise had been correct. The Swamp Witch was, indeed, the witch described by Branfeild in her journal. Everything in that tome was true. Everything.

The Swamp Witch raised a rotted finger, pointed it at The Wraith. "Yes, it is your very soul I covet, for it will be the greatest I have ever gifted my master since that of Eliza Branfeild so long ago. But yours is an even greater prize, one that may yet yield me my long promised reward."

None of this was making any sense to The Wraith, but he could tell that as evil as this witch undoubtedly was, as much pleasure as she clearly derived from her evil, there was something more there. Something...helpless?

The Swamp Witch turned and pointed at the three entangled trees. To The Wraith's amazement, they began to part, like a coiled python unwrapping itself from its prey. "And your Leena is here, too. Her soul is but a morsel compared with yours, but she will serve a purpose, of that you can have no doubt."

Now uncoiled, the abhorrent morass of bark and leaf revealed Leena, unconscious and bound in similar fashion to

The Wraith and Max. She appeared unharmed, but at this distance, he could not be certain.

"What have you done to her!" The Wraith couldn't help but growl. "If you have harmed her in any way—"

"Calm yourself," the Swamp Witch rasped. "She is unharmed...for now. I cannot say for how long, though. That matter is entirely up to you."

"What are you talking about?" The Wraith said, his anger and frustration now overpowering his disgust.

"My master yearns for your soul, it is true, but it must be freely given. You are too powerful for your soul to be of any use to him otherwise. You must give yourself over to me—to him—and only then will your beloved Leena, and your friend Max Horton, be spared. That is the bargain I offer you. But be warned. The alternative is a horror you cannot possibly comprehend."

~ Chapter 13 ~

The Wraith looked over to Max, saw his friend gape in horror at what he was witnessing. A deal with the devil was being offered, with no guarantee of any bond being kept.

"How will I know you will keep your word," The Wraith said, knowing full well the answer. In truth, he was stalling, biding his time. For what, he did not know.

"You do not," the Swamp Witch said. "But what choice do you have? Either you give yourself to me, in the hope that I will hold to our bargain or...you do not wish the consequences in store for you all if you do not surrender."

The Wraith grunted, violently thrashed about, hoping against hope his bindings would weaken, loosen enough to allow him to break free. It was a forlorn hope.

"You are stalling," the witch rasped. "But it will avail you nothing. You hold no bargaining power over me. Your power is as nothing to me. You are not now, nor have you ever been, a match for me."

The Wraith hung his head in despair. Never before had he been so outmatched, so powerless to combat such evil. Not against the Cobra or Aztekoth or Dr. Satanish. Not even against Robert Latham. He must submit. But there was still one chance. Once chance to save Leena and Max, the two people he cared about more than anything in the world. But in order to do so, he needed to acquiesce, to bring the witch closer to him. To begin the process he most dreaded.

"You...win," The Wraith said in a low, resigned voice. "Do as you will with me, but I beg of you...spare Leena and Max."

"No!" Max screamed. "Don't do it! You mustn't!"

"It's all right, Max," The Wraith said calmly, turning to face his friend. "I know what I'm doing...what must be done." He turned to face the hideous Swamp Witch once again. "You will keep your word?"

She cackled. "They will be safe, but do not tarry. I cannot guarantee their safety for long."

Then the witch began to advance, inching her way toward The Wraith. She glided across the water eerily, the tattered ends of her dress skittering through the pond like the legs of the thousands of insects that inhabited the forest. She moved slowly, menacingly; the ripples caused by her movement arrived at the shore before her. She was savoring the moment, as though she was tormenting the two of them before her final moment of success.

In moments, the Swamp Witch was closely approaching The Wraith. Out of the water, she appeared much taller than earlier. The sight and smell of her decomposing body caused him to wretch and gag. She opened her arms in a mockery of a loved one's embrace.

"Paul," she hissed, "come to me..."

The Wraith choked as the Swamp Witch opened her mouth and a ghastly odor emanated from within. He hacked and gagged as she began to press her maggot-filled face towards his. His gaze was drawn to her eyes. They were totally black, but not as in the color itself, but as though they were without color. Twin pools of a void, of nothingness, drawing in everything around them, like a black hole. Pulling at him with tremendous force. He felt his vision begin to blur, the same nothingness beginning to obscure everything around him. The witch wrapped her dead arms around his torso in a perversion of a lover's caress.

"Leena!" Max cried at the top of his lungs. The Wraith could hear him, recognize who it was, and yet...he no longer cared, he no longer had the will to resist.

The Wraith opened his eyes a little, could see the Swamp Witch was less than a foot away. She grasped him by his shoulders, holding him against the tree. She again opened her mouth wide and a milky fog started to emerge from The Wraith's mouth. The Wraith felt his strength draining, his will weakening.

His plan was failing.

All was lost.

Leena let out a scream. She had awoken. Again, The Wraith heard it, but it was somehow muffled, distant.

"Paul!" Leena screamed.

Paul felt a stirring inside him, his will beginning to find an ember of strength.

It can't end like this. It won't.

The Swamp Witch ceased her actions, turned to face the imprisoned Leena. "Silence, wench. Your time will soon come."

This gave The Wraith just enough to regain some measure of composure, some strength. The Eyes of Judgment blazed to life. "Now, Witch, your time of judgment is at hand!"

~ Chapter 14 ~

The Swamp Witch let out a shriek and stumbled backwards. The power of the Eyes of Judgment was enough to trouble her. She lifted a rotted arm in an attempt to shield her vision from the Eyes' glare.

A renewed strength filled The Wraith's limbs, giving them a new purpose. His mind was clear and alert once more. He clenched his fists, anger fueling him. "I have had enough of...swamps." He grabbed hold of the vines that bound his hands and with a singular mighty yank, ripped them from the tree, freeing him. The vines withered the second they were separated from their host, and The Wraith brushed them off his wrists with ease. He did likewise with the vines on his legs. He glared at the Swamp Witch, who was now back at the shore of her pond, shaking, teetering on the edge. The Wraith, his Judgment Stare still active, advanced toward her.

"Foul denizen of evil," The Wraith proclaimed, "now is your end."

"No!" the Swamp Witch gasped, falling to her knees. "It's not possible. How do you resist me? How do you defy me?"

The Wraith ignored her as she stood in undead shock and confusion. Instead, he leapt towards Max and tore at his bindings. In moments, he, too, was free.

"Help Leena," The Wraith told Max.

Max nodded and The Wraith turned his attention back to the Swamp Witch, who was now kneeling in the shallow water whimpering some meaningless gibberish, her face in her hands.

"Now, Witch," The Wraith boomed. "It is time for your soul to...burn!" The Eyes of Judgment took on a new intensity, as though they knew they were facing an evil of unspeakable horror and power.

The Swamp Witch cowered there, her head bowed, hidden beneath her hands. Then, suddenly, she flailed out with her left arm as though beckoning to the surrounding trees. A mighty branch appeared as if from nowhere, swinging down toward the Dread Avenger. The Wraith saw the attack coming in his peripheral vision. He managed to twist his body to one side, just managing to avoid the attack in full, but the branch caught him a glancing blow and he fell hard to the ground. He winced in pain and his ribs burned with intense pain.

"I will not be taken so easily," the Swamp Witch hissed, getting to her feet. "Your soul will yet be mine."

She flailed her arms around in strange and arcane ways; two massive tentacles of vines erupted from the swamp ground on either side of her as if in answer to her calls. The vines were enmeshed like a mighty muscle and tendons. The ends of the vines opened up as though they were the mouths of some gigantic bird of prey.

The Wraith watched in horror as the Swamp Witch directed those vile perversions of nature toward him. They proceeded to attack. The left tentacle struck first and The Wraith had to almost bend all the way backwards in order to avoid being hit as it whooshed over him and plunged into the dirt behind him. He had less than a second before the next tentacle swiped at him. This time The Wraith vaulted over the tentacle as though it was a pommel horse. He landed in a crouch and turned just in time to see the first tentacle turn around and lunge for him again. The Wraith just barely rolled out of the way in time; the tentacle smashed into the tree behind him.

The Wraith had barely gotten to his feet before he was forced to dodge again, diving to the ground as the second tentacle struck at him. He had barely been fast enough. He whirled as he got to his feet, just in time to see both tentacles rushing towards him like two arms reaching out, trying to grab and devour him with their mouths wide open. He had seconds before they would ram into him. He waited. And waited.

At the very last moment, The Wraith leapt onto one of the attacking tentacles, landing on its viny surface. The other tentacle tried to pry him free but the Dread Avenger swerved and bobbed, holding on for dear life as the tentacle he was on wildly thrashed about. The Wraith waited for the right moment, and when he judged the vine's position to be just so, he flung himself from it, launching himself at speed at the Swamp Witch. At such velocity, she was not even able to raise her arms in some meager form of defense.

The Wraith slammed into his quarry with great force, his fist connecting with her face with such power it sent her careening back toward the far end of the swampy pond. The

Wraith rolled and crouched, ready for whatever would come next.

The Swamp Witch struggled to her feet, hissed at him, revealing her horrifying new visage. Several yellow and blackened teeth were now missing. The beak-like nose was broken and it oozed black sludge down her face where blood should have flown. His blow seemed to have shifted her face, as if it had somehow become misaligned. She spat out a tooth in fury.

"You shall pay for this indignity," the Swamp Witch said in sibilant fashion. "I will peel the flesh from your bones and drink from your soul as your life blood ebbs away as your loved one's watch on."

Her hands pulsed with a black energy and the water around her began to bubble and froth, the sand and mud being pushed to the surface by something that was pulling itself up from the depths.

Three bark-skinned tree-like creatures burst from the murky water around the witch. They were at least seven feet tall, their bark covered in mud and a viscous green slime. They growled lowly and terrifyingly as they shrugged off larger clumps of mud and rocks while they stood. Then, in perfect synchronization, they turned to the Swamp Witch, who pointed to The Wraith. The creatures fixed their wooden glares on him and let out inhuman moans. They turned and began their unholy advance toward the Dread Avenger.

The first of the three jumped towards The Wraith and tried to tackle him linebacker style. The Wraith crouched down then propelled himself up and threw his shoulder into the creature's midsection, sending it tumbling over him.

The second creature attacked less than a second later and swiped at The Wraith with its splintered claws. He sidestepped this attack and thrust out his palm. It made direct contact with the creature's midsection; the creature fell backwards, having the wind effectively knocked out of it.

The third creature attacked, coming at The Wraith with a growling intensity, charging, madly swinging its arms about. The Wraith ducked under the first swipe but the second grazed his shoulder, managing to draw blood through the protection of his suit. As the creature moved to strike again, The Wraith grabbed what served as one of its arms, stopping the blow. Then it moved to strike with its remaining arm. The Wraith caught this one, too, and managed to hold firm despite the creature's strength. The Wraith grunted, gritted his teeth in exertion, but he held tight. It was a stalemate of sorts, neither being able to attack the other. On a hunch, The Wraith activated the Eyes of Judgment, bathed the creature in its cleansing energies, then, with the creature completely off-guard, wrenched the wooden arms from their sockets. The creature fell to the ground, helplessly flailing about.

The Wraith whirled as another of the creatures came charging at him. This time The Wraith was armed. As the thing neared, he brought the severed arms he held, now little more than wooden clubs, up and high then smashed them into his enemy. There was a loud thunk and a crash and an explosion of splinters. The creature fell to the ground in a heap, defeated.

The Wraith heard a growl and turned to face the remaining creature. It stood roughly ten paces from him. The Dread Avenger had one club left; the other had been destroyed in the previous assault. He held it aloft like a sword, ready to do battle with this demonic adversary. The creature let out a guttural roar and blindly rushed at him. He stood his ground, waiting, letting it come to him, ready to strike. The creature dove at him; The Wraith reached up like a pinch-hitter for the Metro City Bluebirds, and–struck. If this was a baseball match, it would have been a homerun.

The creature, or what remained of it, lay still on the ground, vanquished.

~ Chapter 15 ~

The Wraith stood triumphant above the creatures he had slain. He dropped his improvised club to the ground, cracked and splintered. He looked around for signs of Leena and Max but saw no sight of them. Clearly, Max had been successful in freeing her and they were now a safe distance away.

Good, he thought. *This is my battle, and it ends now.*

"Swamp Witch," he cried out. "Let us end this."

"Very well," she replied. "I will end this...for you."

She cackled and raised her arms. Black tendrils shaped like gigantic charcoal worms shot forth from her palms. The Wraith didn't have time to react or comprehend what was happening before he was completely ensnared. The tendrils grabbed onto his limbs and then wrapped around his body again and again, leaving only his neck and head free. He was once again at the mercy of the Swamp Witch.

"It need not have come to this," she hissed as she approached The Wraith. "Had you acquiesced, all would have been well. Now only pain and misery await you and everything you hold dear." She stood before him, caressed his stubbled chin as she spoke. "As you have said...let us end this."

The Wraith let out a grunt of tremendous pain as the black tendrils tightened around him even more. His body was being slowly compacted. His teeth ground together as he fought the pain. He screamed as they tightened further, his battered suit providing him little, if any, protection.

"There is pain, I know," the Swamp Witch said, "but it is only as you deserve. My master must have your soul, and I my reward. Nothing can stop this now."

The witch's eyes flashed and The Wraith was drawn into their void once again. As before, his strength ebbed, his will shrank, his very life force drained away. Worse, he was unable to prevent it. He fought hard, tried to assert his will as best he could, but there was little fight left in him. He couldn't help but let out a painful, primal scream as the witch began to pry his soul from his body. She cackled then roared with laughter as her long-yearned-for plans were finally coming to fruition.

* * * * * *

Max and Leena watched on in horror from behind a large fallen tree.

"Max," Leena whispered, "what do we do? We have to help him."

Max turned to his backpack, frantically searched for something, anything that could be used as a weapon of some sort. Then he remembered, and pulled it from his pack–Eliza Branfeild's flintlock pistol. He just prayed it would still work after all these years.

*   *   *   *   *   *

The Wraith screamed in unending agony as his very being withered away with each passing second. Even the pain of his confinement was as nothing to the anguish he was experiencing from within. He knew death would soon arrive.

BANG!

The Swamp Witch ceased her efforts and The Wraith's inner torment ended. He was still imprisoned by the witch's tendrils, but his mind began to slowly clear once more. She glared down at her chest–and found a gaping hole there. She shrieked, perhaps more in shock than in pain, and whirled. The Wraith followed her gaze. There was Max, holding an ancient pistol aloft.

"That...woman's weapon will avail you nothing," the Swamp Witch hissed, seeming to instantly recognize the pistol's origin. "I will deal with you once I have finished this...tasty morsel."

The Wraith knew this would not delay the witch long, but before anyone could react, he spied Leena rushing at the Swamp Witch and, as she neared, she tossed something at the witch's feet.

"Let my fiancé go, you witch!"

The Wraith knew this was flash powder, an element of Max's creation that was so powerful it could consume anything in seconds. Nothing thus far it encountered was immune to its force. But, at the last second, the Swamp

Witch turned, twisted her body sideways, and managed to avoid the full brunt of the powder. The tendrils were destroyed, part of the witch's left arm, but nothing more. But it was enough. The Wraith was free, landing on the ground in a crouch, his strength and composure returning. He took in several deep breaths. The Swamp Witch staggered back.

"Swamp Witch," The Wraith boomed, his Eyes of Judgment bursting once more into fiery life, "now your judgment will commence. You will pay for your crimes against humanity."

The Eyes crackled with intense electrical energy as The Wraith advanced toward the witch. Her black, empty eyes widened in fear. She stumbled and cowed backwards.

"Your soul will be cleansed even as it is consumed!"

He grabbed her by the shoulders, brought her face up into the path of his Judgment Stare and she shrieked in abject terror.

"Nooooo," she howled, "this cannot be. I am all-powerful. I am time immemorial. You cannot defeat me. Nothing can stop me!"

All further words were lost in a torment of screams as the Swamp Witch broke free of The Wraith's grasp and doubled over in pain. Then, unbelievably, she sprung upright, spewing smoke from her mouth. Fire–unlike any The Wraith had ever seen–sprung from somewhere within her chest and quickly began to spread across her thrashing body. She shrieked and howled as she began to be consumed by the ethereal flames.

The Swamp Witch turned and charged towards the swamp, diving headfirst into the muddy water. When her body broke the surface, there was the sound akin to that of thunder from within the bowels of the earth and a massive geyser of smoke and ash erupted from her point of entry, billowing into the sky. The Wraith, now joined by Leena and Max, could only watch on with incredulity. The water began to hiss and bubble throughout its circumference and a thick, bulbous mist rose, quickly enveloping the three of them.

The Wraith hacked at the acrid taste, the mist both burning his mouth and lungs. Leena and Max, previously just mere feet from him, were now completely obscured by the otherworldly fog.

"Leena!" The Wraith cried out. "Max!"

He heard coughing in reply, two sets, and knew they were both safe and nearby. But where? He couldn't make out a direction, couldn't make heads or tails of his current position or situation. All he could see and feel was fog–an unnatural, mysterious fog.

The Wraith swiveled, tried to get his bearings, tried to ascertain where the audible coughs were coming from. A shape smacked into his back. He whirled to find Max standing there, coughing up a lung but otherwise apparently unharmed. The Wraith took him by the arms.

"Max, where's Leena?"

"She was right beside me when this...stuff erupted. What the hell is going on here? What is this we're breathing in?"

"Leena!" The Wraith shouted again, ignoring Max. "Leena!"

Moments that stretched into minutes that soon felt like hours passed by. Finally, the mist began to slowly, inexorably clear. There, at the edge of the swamp, lay Leena, face down in the shallow water.

"No," The Wraith whispered. He leapt to her side. He got to his knees, carefully rolled her over, and...she slowly sat, opened her eyes, and coughed up water and mud.

"Leena," The Wraith said softly, taking her into his arms. "Are you all right? Take a few deep breaths."

Once the coughing had subsided, she turned to him, tears in her eyes, and they embraced. "Darling. Is it over? Is this nightmare finally over?"

The Wraith looked at her carefully then turned to face Max. He merely shrugged his shoulders. "Yes, I believe so. The Swamp Witch is no more." The roiling water was now beginning to calm and there was no sign of the Swamp Witch in evidence.

"I don't know about you," Max said, joining the two by the edge of the water, "but I'd like to get the heck outta here. I've had it up to here with nature." He indicated a spot on his face.

The Wraith helped Leena to her feet and they both smiled at their friend. "Yes. I think it's time we all returned home."

After a further few moments to compose themselves, they looked about for whatever of their belongings remained, collected them, and started to make their way back toward the trees, out into the forest and, hopefully, toward the path that would lead them back to civilization.

As they entered the nearest copse, Leena stopped abruptly and turned back toward the hellish place they were endeavoring to escape.

"This place..." she began and shuddered.

"And this also...has been one of the dark places of the earth." Max smiled at Leena.

She returned his look with one of confusion. "Sorry, what?"

"Another classical quote for you. Conrad, remember?" Max said, raising an eyebrow

"Oh yes, of course. With all that's happened, I must have forgotten," Leena said as she joined The Wraith amongst the trees.

Max followed her into the forest. In time, the three of them managed to find the path that appeared to be the one they had taken earlier and made their way down it.

~ Chapter 16 ~

As they walked, they soon came across features they recognized—clearings, the cottage, the river, the canyon—that they had traversed earlier and thanked their blessings. Ultimately, the return journey took a few days, but as they moved further and further away from Satan's Forest, the sky began to clear, the weather improved, and the expedition became all the easier.

Their final campsite had been on the spot of their first, now outside the confines of Satan's Forest, this area of forested countryside was beautiful, lush, filled with the sights and sounds of mother nature and, bathed in the last vestiges of the day's sunshine, nourishing for the soul. Something they all needed after their harrowing ordeal.

As they sat, eating what was left of the meager provisions that remained in Max's backpack, Paul took Leena in his arms. "I thought I'd lost you forever," he said.

"I thought the same thing when Max and I lost sight of you."

They kissed, enjoying the touch, sight and smell of each other after so long.

"Let's turn in," Paul said. "One last day of hiking before we reach the car."

Later, they awoke feeling surprisingly refreshed and revitalized. The sun shone bright and they were greeted with the sight of deer milling nearby and a family of squirrels scuttling up and down trees. Fish leapt from an adjacent brook.

Paul stowed his suit in Max's backpack and, breaking camp quickly, they made their way onward. Now that the end was in sight and home was beckoning, their pace was steady and sure. Paul couldn't help but smile. Even the thought of Metro City, as corrupt and dirty a metropolis as anyone could ever find, felt warm and cozy to him now. Almost like putting on an old shoe.

As they strode through the high grass and thickets, they passed the time warmly, chatting about what they would do when they arrived home, planning their wedding, taking (another) break. A proper holiday this time.

And then, after a further few hours of hiking, they came into a clearing, one that was both heartening and frightening at the same time. It was the Pondworthy School parking lot. Not the clearing behind the Bidbury hotel. Nowhere near the area where they had originated from.

"What the..." Max uttered.

"Yet another mystery," Paul said as he pushed his fingers through his hair. "Add it to the list."

There was nothing else for it but to walk–more walking–to the hotel where their car was parked. As they started, Paul stared up at the school ruins and ruminated over their time there. Everything seemed to come back to Satanish. He cursed his inability at capturing such a menace. His thoughts then shifted. What started as a holiday away from the crime and grime of Metro City ended as anything but. They had encountered such evil, such a demonic presence, the mere thought of it caused Paul to shudder. Despite his confidence in his own abilities and in his life's work, he was nevertheless astounded they had managed to get through their recent travails. While confronting such evil had shocked and hardened him, their victories had replenished his soul, strengthened his resolve that their mission was sound and needed.

He moved to place a comforting arm around Leena's shoulder but found she was not standing where she had only moments before. He turned and saw Leena by the edge of the parking lot, staring off back into the woods where they had recently emerged. Curious, he ambled over to her side.

"Leena?" he said softly.

"Hmm...oh, Paul," she said. "I was just...thinking."

Paul placed an arm over her shoulders. "We've been through a lot. Are you okay?"

She turned and smiled at him. "I will be."

He led the way back to the main road. Their destination was still a few miles away but, eventually, they would be back at the Ryan farmhouse and would, finally, be able to rest and recuperate.

*   *   *   *   *   *

Back at the farmhouse, Paul stepped out of the ensuite bathroom wearing sweatpants, still drying his hair. He had showered much longer than usual, but felt the need to fully cleanse every square inch of his body from the muck and filth it had been exposed to. Finally, after much scrubbing, he felt clean again.

"The bathroom's all yours," he called to Leena as she sat on the bed, staring off into space, her back to him. "You could have joined me, you know."

Leena didn't respond but remained silent and unmoving, still wearing the same muddy, disgusting clothes she'd been in all these weeks, and the stench was beginning to build.

"Leena, I think you–" Paul began, but then he stopped; his body went rigid. Every hair on his body stood on end. He watched, speechless and horrified, as Leena turned her head to face him and look him directly in the eye, smiling, while her body remained still and facing the other way.

"Yes, Paul? What is it?" she asked, behaving as if nothing was untoward.

Paul could only gasp at the utter revulsion that drenched his heart, and the dread realization of what this meant.

Leena let out a laugh, shrill and high-pitched. "Oh, did I startle you?" She roared with laughter.

"What...are you?" Paul managed to say.

"Is there something wrong?" Leena asked with an innocent glance.

"Where is Leena?" Paul demanded, regaining his composure as best he could. "What have you done with her?"

"Oh, I would have thought that obvious by now," Leena said, her head straightening out. She stood and slowly her body began to shift, to change before Paul's eyes. A few moments later, where Leena had once been, now stood a creature that almost resembled a tree, though unlike any tree that existed in nature. Its skin was bark-like, rough and stubbly, with stony hooves in place of feet, and atop its head was hair that was string-like and mossy. Its face was contorted with wickedness.

"Where is she?" Paul demanded again.

"Back in the swamp where you abandoned her," the creature said with glee. "In the waiting arms of my mistress."

The implication was obvious though it galled him to admit it. "The Swamp Witch," he whispered.

"Yes," the creature cackled. "My mistress lives. She is everlasting."

His fury building, Paul vaulted the bed as he rushed the creature, extending his foot out. It caught the creature squarely in the face, sending it reeling back into an adjacent dresser. Paul landed in a crouch and before the creature could recover, he charged it again. This time he body-slammed it into the dresser and the creature's mossy head snapped backwards, shattering the mirror at the top. Shards of glass fell around the two of them. Before the creature could strike back, Paul pinned its arms to its side and pushed his face within inches of the creature's.

"If any harm has come to Leena..." Paul grunted.

"Oh, but it undoubtedly has," the creature said with much joy. "My mistress hungers for souls. She devours them as you would food. In your absence, she was eager for nourishment."

Furious beyond words, Paul smashed the creature into the bedroom wall to his left. Splinters burst forth upon impact.

"You are too late," the creature said. "Your Leena is gone. Gone!"

"No!" Paul said. He charged the creature once again. This time they careened out through the bedroom door into the farmhouse's living room. They wrestled there, the creature trying to break free from Paul's grip. Then, the home's front door opened, with Max appearing in the entryway.

"I'm back," he said, clearly not yet noticing the titanic struggle taking place before him. "I thought I'd take a look at the–" Max stopped in his tracks.

"Max!" Paul cried, fighting for his life, "stay back."

Max did as instructed but appeared ready to enter the fray.

"You are powerless to save her," the creature said. "She will already have proven a tasty morsel for my mistress."

It swiped at Paul with a wooden claw, drawing blood on his bare chest. Paul wiped at his wound, took a few strategic steps back, and contemplated his next move. He yearned for his suit, his belt, for some handy flash powder. He had his Eyes of Judgment, of course, but he now doubted their efficacy in dealing with supernatural adversaries.

As he pondered, the creature took the advantage, swiping some more with its deadly claws. Paul managed to swerve, then ducked this way and that, avoiding further injury. This would have to be a battle of strength and brains. He lashed out with a powerful right, connecting with the creature's face, but cried out in pain as splinters embedded in his hand.

The creature, its face mottled and shredded, leered at him. "My fate is irrelevant. The battle is already won."

Paul, despite the pain, smashed his fist into his opponents face again and again, reducing it to mere rubble. It staggered back, severely harmed but still able to cause damage, to fight back. Paul was now too angry to feel pain and he pressed forward, eager to end it.

"Chief!" Max shouted, appearing suddenly from the front door. The burly Irishman lunged past his friend toward the creature. "Take cover!"

Max hurled a pellet at the creature's feet and, before it even knew what was happening, the flash powder took its deadly toll. Before it was all over, the creature howled in defiance. In seconds, it was gone, utterly consumed.

Paul and Max stood, the pain from Paul's chest wound and his battered right hand now coming to the fore. Paul turned his right hand over, examined the wound. His knuckles were completely torn up, bleeding freely, and splinters–large and small–were in clear evidence. He didn't care.

"Chief, you're hurt," Max said, moving over to his friend.

"It's nothing." Paul waved him away. "We have to go back. Leena's still out there."

Max gasped at the shock of Paul's words. "But..."

"No buts," Paul said, marching back to the bedroom to retrieve his suit. "Leena's life is at stake. Nothing else matters."

Max followed him into the bedroom, rubbed at his chin. "I'll get the car started."

~ Chapter 17 ~

The Wraith ran as fast as he could through the woods. He had much terrain to cover and very little time to cover it. Leena's life–perhaps her soul–truly was at stake. He only hoped he wouldn't be too late, that it wasn't too late already.

He could only hope and pray.

He rounded tree after tree, recognized such natural landscapes as streams and clearings, and knew he was on the right path. Even at his top speed, with his lungs burning, he knew it would take days to reach the heart of Satan's Forest, and even with his stamina, his powerful will, he would eventually need to slow, to rest. The thought sickened him, and he pressed on.

Hours passed, but he knew that even the outermost perimeter of Satan's Forest was still a long distance away. He pushed himself harder and further than he had ever done before. His lungs boiled, his muscles ached, his many wounds throbbed with concentrated pain. He pushed all such feelings aside. All that mattered was Leena.

As dusk approached, the sun starting to disappear behind tree and hillside, the edge of Satan's Forest now lay before him. Without thought, he plunged inside and a gloomy darkness surrounded him. The light dimmed dramatically, all sight and sound of animal life vanished, and the forest itself took on a mysterious, otherworldly hue.

He had made excellent time, better than even he had thought possible, but he was now starting to weary and his pace forcibly slackened. He pushed himself on, but he was no longer able to keep up his speed. He cursed the fates for his perceived weakness.

A massive boulder up ahead loomed large, blocking the path forward.

I don't remember this. Have I taken the wrong path?

He looked up and around, frantically searching for any recognizable point of reference...but nothing looked familiar. He was lost, perhaps hopelessly so.

He didn't dare turn back, so he pressed on, circled the boulder...and found himself back in the Swamp Witch's lair, at the swampy clearing, the water roiling gently as though in anticipation of his arrival.

The Wraith knew there was demonic sorcery at work here. This place, by all rights, should still have been days away, and here he now was. He was clearly expected. Yet, there was no sign of the Swamp Witch. Or of Leena. The entrance to the cave lay at the opposite end of the swamp. A gurgling, ominous tone was still emanating from it as before but this time louder, more pronounced. Yes, he was expected. He would not disappoint the witch.

There was no way to circumvent the swampy pond–trees and the thick brush that grew right up to the water's edge on either side. Only the way before him was free. His path, therefore, was clear. Into the murky water he trudged, his footsteps causing the unnatural liquid to churn and bubble. It was only ankle deep to start but soon deepened to around waist high, but no deeper. His onward trek was slow; the mud underfoot was thick and sticky. Each forward step became a mighty struggle, but nothing would stop his march to destiny. Leena's fate depended on him.

Ultimately, he reached the mouth of the cave and, what had previously appeared to be a stream entering it, deepened markedly into something akin to that of a narrow river. A fetid, sewer-like river. He could no longer walk and was forced to swim, breaststroke, into the cave.

The cave narrowed into a slender tunnel, not much wider than the river, and pitch dark. The Wraith reached up to his temple and activated his night-vision lenses. Surprisingly, they were now working in this demonic realm place. The tunnel brightened into visibility. The walls of the cavern surrounding him were covered in eerie formations, almost resembling pustules, and the smell was worsening with each stroke of his arms. Even with his night-vision lenses, he could not see far in front of him. Despite the wonders of modern technology, the darkness that lay beyond was too overbearing, too sinister, to fully illuminate.

As he continued into the darkness, the river again began to shallow and he was able to touch bottom and walk once more. First shoulder high, then waist, then the water receded back down to his ankles.

The stench was now almost unbearable. The Wraith realized it wasn't just his surrounds but the water itself. The stink now came from himself as much as anything else. He could no longer control his gag reflex and, not wishing to delay his progress any further, reached down to his belt and pulled from it his rebreather. Placing it in his mouth, he savored the clean, pure oxygen now flooding into his lungs. He knew it wouldn't last long but took advantage of it and hurried forward through the water and mud.

Finally, some distance in front of him started to become clear through his lenses and he was certain he was nearing his goal. The water underfoot was now little more than a trickle, as though a schoolyard faucet had been left slightly open. He rushed onward. Up ahead, the tunnel became blocked by what appeared to be some sort of curtain, though crafted from twigs instead of fabric. Upon reaching it, The Wraith pushed it aside and was met with a sight of sheer, unmitigated horror.

The tunnel dramatically opened into a large, cylindrical cavern. Stalactites unlike any he had seen before burst from every available space around him, corpses—in various degrees of decomposition—impaled on almost every one of them. It was a house of horrors, of sheer insanity, and The Wraith struggled to contain his emotions. The sight and smell of this environment would be enough to send a person mad.

An ordinary person, perhaps, but the Dread Avenger was no ordinary person. Sickened beyond belief, he nevertheless held firm, his resolve all-powerful.

Up ahead, large stalagmites shot upward, like gigantic teeth vying for attention with the stalactites above. Further bodies were mingled in amongst these stony columns but still no sign of life. All about him was only death.

Frantic, he hunted around him. His beloved Leena had to be there somewhere. All could not yet be lost. She was not hanging above, staked like victims of history's Vlad Tepes of Romania. Nor was she lying amongst the human debris neighboring the stony pillars he now coursed through.

Where are you, Leena?

He continued his search. Some moments later, he stopped in his tracks. His quest was over. There, bound to a smooth, jutting pillar, was the motionless body of Leena Patterson.

He rushed to her, tried to rouse her, but she was unresponsive. She appeared unharmed but was covered in putrid muck and filth. He cut her from her binds and gently cradled her in his arms.

"Leena," he whispered and gave her a kiss.

She was breathing, but only barely. She was cold to the touch and as pale as death. He quickly wrapped her in his cape and held her, trying to get her warm. He rubbed at her limbs, trying to speed the process, but knew not what else to do. He prayed she would be all right.

In time, her breathing strengthened, she felt warmer to the touch, and her color started to return. She slowly opened her eyes, and The Wraith thanked the Lord.

"P...Paul..." Leena gasped.

"I'm here, darling. You're going to be okay."

Leena's eyes opened wide in terror.

"Paul!" she cried out.

There was a slight sound...something–or someone–was behind him. He whirled.

There was the Swamp Witch, alive and well, dripping with vengeful fury.

~ Chapter 18 ~

Yes, the Swamp Witch lived, but she was much diminished. Her arm was still missing, the gaping hole in her chest remained, and her rotted hair and skin was blackened by the energy of The Wraith's Judgment Stare. He noted this and knew then he had the power to vanquish her.

But the Swamp Witch, despite her injuries, was still a force to be reckoned with. With surprising speed, she ran forward, grabbed The Wraith by the shoulder and flung him the length of the cave. He sailed through the air until he crashed into a stalagmite, landing in a heap of stony fragments and body parts.

"You have fallen into my trap," the Swamp Witch cackled. "Neither of you will leave this place alive."

She held her sole arm aloft and black tendrils shot forth, The Wraith their intended target. This time, he was able to dodge their deadly grasp. He rolled to one side. The tendrils slammed into the stalagmite where he had once been and vanished upon impact.

The Wraith tensed his body in readiness to continue the battle when he saw Leena had crept behind the Swamp Witch and now launched herself onto the witch's back. She reached her arms around the witch's neck, gripping her in a tight headlock. They struggled there for a moment, but the Swamp Witch reached up with her good arm, grabbed Leena by the hair, and yanked her up and over, flinging Leena to the ground with much force.

"Leena," The Wraith couldn't help but cry out.

"She will soon perish," the Swamp Witch hissed, "and you will then follow. Enough games!"

The Wraith agreed with her. He'd had enough. This would end now.

The Eyes of Judgment flared to brilliant life once again and The Wraith did not hesitate to press forward the advantage. The Swamp Witch's confidence drained away, and she backed up as he advanced toward her.

"This truly is your end, foul witch," The Wraith boomed. "No more escape for you. Judgment will be administered."

In desperation, she lashed out once again with her tendrils, but they fizzled and were rent asunder in the blazing energies of the Eyes of Judgment. The Wraith would not be deterred. Judgment would no longer be denied. He continued his steady advance.

"No," the Swamp Witch said. "My reward was so near, my release was almost upon me."

As The Wraith closed on his prey, he finally noticed a small, gold medallion hanging around the witch's neck. It was filthy and tarnished, but some of the gold still gave off a slight glint. And there, at its center, was a tiny cross with the initials E.B. below it. He gasped at the sight of it. Didn't

Leena say this was worn by a corpse in a small cottage in another part of the forest? Nothing made sense. The Witch noticed his confusion and, despite her predicament, smiled salaciously.

"You no doubt think I stole this, took it from the very body of Eliza Branfeild," she hissed. "You fool. Do you not yet realize the truth–I *am* Eliza Branfeild!"

The Eyes of Judgment petered out. The Wraith stopped in his tracks, shocked beyond all meaning. He couldn't make sense of the situation. Nothing felt as it should. Could it be that the Branfeild journal was somehow a fake? Could the Swamp Witch have been playing with them all, with their dreams, the entire time? Or was this merely another trick? Another malicious attempt to seed confusion and mayhem?

She again attacked with her lethal tendrils. This time The Wraith was caught off guard, too slow and close to avoid them, and was trapped in their vicelike grip once more.

"No more holy flame," she hissed as she brought him close to her. "No more judgment. Now it is my turn. Salvation will soon be at hand."

She opened her repulsive mouth, moved to suck the lifeforce from his body. It was over. All was lost.

"Arrrggggghhhh!"

Leena appeared as if from nowhere, leaping into the fray, brandishing a large femur bone in her hands. She brought the weapon down hard on the witch's head, causing the creature to step back and loosen her grip. Not allowing the witch a moment to recover, Leena drove the bone through the Swamp Witch's head, driving it in with such force it burst through the monster's face, sending rotting flesh and a black ooze gushing out over The Wraith. He coughed and sputtered the sickening fluid away as best he could. The Swamp Witch staggered back, severely wounded, reached up to her face in an attempt to remove the bony protrusion.

The Wraith, now free, knew he had to act quickly. He let loose with a spinning scissor kick, catching the witch square in the torso. Blinded, and wounded as she was, she had no hope of avoiding the blow. She was flung backward, crashing into a stalagmite and landing in a heap on the ground.

With her face completely mutilated, The Wraith briefly wondered whether his Judgment Stare would now be effective. He decided not to chance it, not to give the Swamp Witch even the remotest ability to recover and start the battle anew. This had to end *now*.

The Wraith reached to his belt, retrieved two flash pellets–an extra one for good measure–and lobbed them directly at his adversary. Helpless, flailing about amongst the human flotsam, the Swamp Witch didn't know what hit her. In a blinding flash, the two pellets hit their target, and she cried out in unending agony.

"Noooooooooo!"

It was over in seconds. The witch's body writhed and contorted in pain as she was utterly consumed. In moments, all that remained was ashes.

Leena ran to The Wraith's side.

"Is it...truly over?" she said.

"I think so," The Wraith said.

He took her in his arms. In those moments that followed, nothing else mattered. They had each other.

And that was enough.

~ Epilogue ~

Days later, Paul and Leena were seated in the morning room of their Sanderson House home. The sun shone brightly through the expansive bay window, bathing them in a golden hue that was most welcome after what they had recently been through.

The butler Simpson entered, carrying a tray with a silver coffee pot and some cups. "Will Master Max be joining you?"

"Yes, I think I will, Simpson," Max said as he entered the room, his face beaming. He joined Paul and Leena in a chair by the window.

"Thank you, Simpson. I'll pour," Paul said.

Simpson exited and Paul proceeded to pour each of them a steaming cup of the finest, Vittoria coffee. They sat in silence for a few moments, letting the warm liquid fortify them, before Max spoke up.

"Chief...there's something I don't understand." Max paused, his face knotted in confusion.

"Go on, Max," Paul said.

"Well," the Irishman began, "the Swamp Witch claiming to be Eliza Branfeild. That doesn't jibe with what was written in the Branfeild journal. Clearly that monster was bedeviling the area long before Branfeild got there."

Paul leaned forward on the couch, happy to relate his theories. "I suspect Branfeild was just another victim of the Swamp Witch. She was, as we all bore witness, a devourer of souls. Perhaps that is what the witch meant."

Max took a sip of coffee, seeming to be mulling over the point.

"However," Paul said, "I did spend yesterday checking some of the names and dates mentioned in the journal and many of them are either inaccurate or complete falsehoods, at least as far as I was able to determine. Whether that's a result of Branfeild misremembering–if they're true, she was under great duress when she wrote many of those entries–or they were outright fabrications by the witch herself, who knows?"

Leena gasped slightly at this.

"But...the dreams, hallucinations..." Max said.

"Could well have been just the Swamp Witch toying with us, messing with our minds. She was a master of manipulation so she certainly was capable of such," Paul said.

Max looked to Leena, then back to Paul.

"I don't think we'll ever know the full truth of the matter," Paul said. "And, I suppose, it doesn't really matter in the end."

Max scratched at the back of his neck. He clearly was still troubled by it all.

"Anyway," Leena said, changing the subject, "what about that marriage proposal, Mr. Sanderson. We now have a wedding to plan you know."

Paul squirmed a little in his seat. While he was more than eager to marry the love of his life, the organizing of it all was something that made his skin crawl. "Ahh...whatever you want, go for it. You have my complete trust to plan it all to your heart's content."

Leena didn't appear to be too happy with that answer, but she said nothing further. She took another sip of coffee instead.

"Well, I'll leave you two lovebirds alone to debate that," Max said as he placed his empty cup back on the nearby tray and stood. "I've got to get back to work. I have to restock your belt, Chief, and get started on those backup suits."

And with that, and a doff of his cap, he was off.

Leena drained her cup also and placed it back on the tray. "I can see where Max is coming from. It's hard not knowing the full extent of what we experienced out there in Satan's Forest. What was real and what wasn't."

Paul nodded. "In researching Bidbury, I found no mention of a rash of missing people at any point in its history. There was an Eliza Branfeild, but there's very little written about her, making it impossible to verify anything."

Leena looked concerned. "What does all that mean?"

Paul shrugged his shoulders. "Perhaps there was no written account of whatever might have happened in Bidbury around that time, or it's been lost to the ravages of time, or it was somehow covered up by..."

"Or it never happened at all, or at least not as the journal claims it did," Leena added.

"That's the mystery, and there's no real way of determining the truth at this point," Paul said. "I guess what matters most is the area is, finally, safe. You saw Satan's Forest once we emerged from that cave. The gloomy atmosphere was gone. The people of Bidbury and the surrounding area can now get on with their lives. As can we." He moved in close to her. "What was that about organizing a wedding?"

*   *   *   *   *   *

Dr. Satanish brooded alone in his darkened quarters. His plans for conquest, for freeing his demonic master, lay in tatters. For the first time in as long as he could remember, he was aimless, totally without purpose.

The Wraith. He is responsible for my travails.

He was consumed with a burning desire for vengeance, for some sort of plan to make The Wraith pay for his defiance. But nothing came. He wracked his brain, turned over this scenario and that, but nothing sounded right. Nothing was really...then it hit him. Vultures. He had his serum, had his equipment. And, above all, his genius. It would take time. Much time. But nothing would stop his plan from progressing.

Oh yes, how delicious.

It was perfect. Simply perfect. He would start at once. Nothing would prevent his revenge.

Metro City would serve as the ultimate prize.

~ Author's Note ~

I'm very proud of this story, both in its overall quality and for the very fact that it is finally here, after all these years.

Swamp Witch of Satan's Forest was always the intended follow-up to the novel, *Cry of the Werewolf.* That novel was first published in 2012, and I was already well advanced in the writing of *Swamp Witch* at that time, fully intending to release it within a year or two of its predecessor. But then I hit a wall. After a few chapters in, I just did not know how to proceed with the story. Call it writer's block, call it what you will, but I just found it impossible to proceed. So, I let it lie, hoping (expecting?) to be able to get back to it before too long. But the ideas never came, and I thought up new Wraith books and plotlines and advanced those in the meantime. I also thought to, perhaps, publish *Swamp Witch* as a series of short stories instead. In the end, the project languished as I went on with other stories.

Finally, 2023 came, and I was determined to move forward with my original plans to advance *Swamp Witch* as a novel. However, the ideas for the story were still shrouded in mystery, so I knew I needed help. Hence my esteemed, and super-talented co-writer, Ray MacKay, came to my rescue. He used my initial chapters and overall plot ideas, and fashioned a masterful story of horror and thrills unlike any The Wraith has ever encountered before. His brilliant work fired my imagination, and enabled me to take his first draft manuscript and to shape it into what you now have before you. I can never thank him enough.

So, to those thanks...obviously, to Ray MacKay, for his invaluable help in finishing this story. To my wife, Jennifer, and our daughter, Emma...you are my inspiration. To my family and friends and, to all my fans and readers...thank you for hanging in there with me after all these years. Your support has nurtured me and fuelled me to continue with this series of stories. There are more–many more–to come, I assure you.

Take care
Frank Dirscherl
Wollongong, 2025

~ Also Available ~

The Wraith Dread Avenger of the Underworld #1
THE WRAITH
Frank Dirscherl

In a world not far removed from our own, a city lies ravaged.
Crime overruns its streets, its citizens are helpless. Crime lord
Robert Latham holds the city in his sway. One man, however,
stands above the rest, willing to fight for freedom. That man is
The Wraith!

NOW AVAILABLE!

www.glowingeyesmedia.com

The Wraith Dread Avenger of the Underworld #3
CROSSFIRE
Stephen J. Semones & Frank Dirscherl

After a terrorist attack leaves the citizens of Metro City reeling, an enigmatic stranger emerges from the wake of the destruction to wage war on local crime-lord Robert Latham. In the midst of this, Max Horton, The Wraith's right-hand man, vanishes without a trace. Searching for Max, and for those responsible for the devastation, The Wraith sets out for answers.

NOW AVAILABLE!

www.glowingeyesmedia.com

The Wraith Dread Avenger of the Underworld #5
CRY OF THE WEREWOLF
Frank Dirscherl

Having gone through ordeal after ordeal, Paul Sanderson (aka The Wraith Dread Avenger of the Underworld ®) and his love Leena Patterson, decide to take a long overdue vacation. However, their idyll is soon shattered by an attack by a creature nobody thought could possibly exist—a werewolf. Soon, an evil so heinous makes himself known, and only The Wraith could possibly defeat it.

NOW AVAILABLE!

www.glowingeyesmedia.com

The Wraith Dread Avenger of the Underworld #8
LADY WRAITH
Frank Dirscherl & Adam Oravec

The Wraith is missing. No one has seen him since going out on patrol. Now, the love of his life Leena Patterson, must sally forth on her own as Lady Wraith, protect the city, find her love, and combat a deadly new adversary hell-bent on destruction.

COMING SOON!

www.glowingeyesmedia.com

Books of Judgment Book One
SANDERSON OF METRO
Frank Dirscherl & Bobby Nash

Two masters of the pulp fiction world, Frank Dirscherl and Bobby
Nash, have come together to tell this tale, the secret NEVER before
told origin of the first Wraith/Paul Sanderson, as only they could.
This action-packed, atmospheric thrill could only be told now, and
it could only be told by master storytellers like Dirscherl and
Nash. An epic never to be repeated and not to be missed.

NOW AVAILABLE!

www.glowingeyesmedia.com

Books of Judgment Book Two
SERPENT RISING
Frank Dirscherl & Greg Gick

The never-before-told origin story of The Wraith's arch nemesis the Cobra. Who he is, how he came to be, and how his and the original Paul Sanderson's life intertwined at key moments to cause them to become deadly adversaries. It's all here!

NOW AVAILABLE!

www.glowingeyesmedia.com

About the Type

Garamond is a group of many old-style serif typefaces, originally those designed by Parisian craftsman Claude Garamond and other 16th century French engravers, and now many modern revivals. Though his name was written as 'Garamont' in his lifetime, the typefaces are generally spelled 'Garamond'. **Garamond Normal**, used in this book, is one of those modern revivals.

Join FRANK DIRSCHERL and Glowing
Eyes Media on social media!

facebook.com/glowingeyesmedia

@glowingeyesmedia

instagram.com/glowingeyesmedia

glowingeyesmedia.proboards.com

All Glowing Eyes Media, The Wraith and Starflame
novels, comics and merchandise can be obtained
directly from the Glowing Eyes Media website –
www.glowingeyesmedia.com

Want to be The Wraith?

Well, it might be hard to actually *be* The Wraith, unless of course you, too, have been endowed with the power of the Eyes of Judgment. But you can certainly dress, drink and drive like him [*] (and you don't always have to be a millionaire to do so). See for yourselves.

The Wraith/Paul Sanderson wears:

- tailored clothing from Cad & the Dandy Tailors and Shirtmakers – www.cadandthedandy.co.uk
- bespoke footwear from Gaziano & Girling – www.gazianogirling.com
- watches from Héron (Marinor in Atlantic Blue) -

www.heronwatches.com/collections/marinor/products/marinor-atlantic-blue
- Armani Code cologne from Giorgio Armani – www.giorgioarmanibeauty-usa.com/for-him-armani-code/for-him-armani-code,default,sc.html

drinks:

- Twinings Earl & Lady Grey tea – www.twinings.co.uk
- Vittoria coffee – www.vittoriacoffee.com/

---

[*] Please note: Glowing Eyes Media does not condone drinking and driving. **All** adults, please always drink responsibly and **never** drink and drive

- The Balvenie Scotch whisky – www.thebalvenie.com
- Armand de Brignac champagne – www.armanddebrignac.com
- Cosmopolitan cocktails

uses:

- Dell laptops – www.dell.com.au
- Chesterfield furniture from Abbey Furniture www.chesterfieldfurnituremelbourne.com.au
- wallets from Launer – www.launer.com
- a Samsung Galaxy J5 Pro cell phone – www.samsung.com/latin_en/smartphones/galaxy-j5-2017/SM-J530GZDITPA/

drives:

- a Rolls Royce Wraith – www.rolls-roycemotorcars.com/en-GB/wraith.html

And, if you're really eager to actually look like The Wraith—in full costume—then you can always head over to Xtreme Design FX and let Lance Coulter there make you an exact replica of the costume used for The Wraith motion picture – www.xtremedesignfx.com

HÉRON

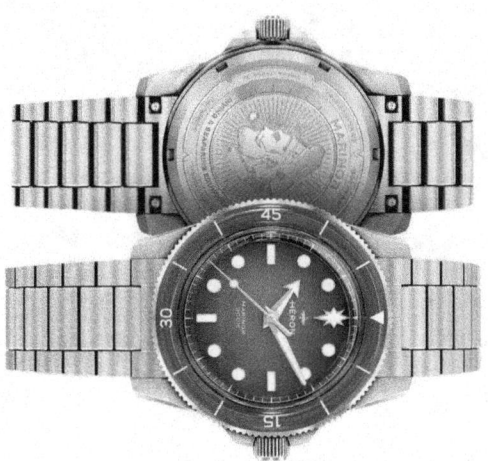

Héron Marinor in Atlantic Blue - The Watch For Superheroes

www.ingramcontent.com/pod-product-compliance
Lightning Source LLC
Chambersburg PA
CBHW070523260626
47161CB00004B/1623